A TALENT
TO DECEIVE

A TALENT
TO DECEIVE

•

Denisa Nickell
Hanania

AVALON BOOKS
NEW YORK

Published by Thomas Bouregy & Co., Inc.
160 Madison Avenue, New York, NY 10016

Library of Congress Cataloging-in-Publication Data

Hanania, Denisa Nickell.
    A talent to deceive / Denisa Nickell Hanania.
        p. cm.
    ISBN 978-0-8034-9859-4 (acid-free paper)
    I. Title.

PS3608.A6765T35 2007
813'.6—dc22

                                    2007016637

PRINTED IN THE UNITED STATES OF AMERICA
ON ACID-FREE PAPER
BY HADDON CRAFTSMEN, BLOOMSBURG, PENNSYLVANIA

To my loving husband, Marwan Hanania, who never raises an eyebrow when he takes me out for a romantic dinner and I mutter, "This would be a great place to stash a dead body."

To our sons, Dan, Max, Elijah, Caleb, Nicholas, and Tommy. You are the true characters in my life.

All glory and praise to Jesus Christ, the author and finisher of my faith.

The real Ladies of the Club in order of appearance:

Donna Kreke—you are the most genuine person I know. Lara's down to earth logic and her ability to always come through were born in you.

Gabriele Christie—your constant loyalty, legendary organizational skills, and fireball energy provided the very essence for Romy. According to my lawyers, however, Romy did *NOT* get her lock picking abilities from you.

Diana Nikou—our Club Southern Belle. Your gracious, loving spirit inspired Grace's generosity and compassion just as you always inspire me.

"And say my glory was I had such friends." William Butler Yeats, Irish dramatist & poet (1865–1939)

With love and gratitude to my parents, Ken and Esther Nickell. Your encouragement and faith in me laid the foundation for everything I achieve.

To Karen Artrip, Bobbie Campbell, Carla Pelfrey, Betty Russell, Carla Stoneberg, Stephanie Terry, and PJ Tierney. Thank you for your suggestions and encouragement. *A Talent to Deceive* is better because of your critiques.

Celina is a blend of two very special friends—Gwen Brewer and Stephanie Terry.

Stephanie provided the role model for Celina's beauty along with her uncanny sense for reading people. Celina inherited Gwen's cool ability to remain poised and her amazing analytical skills. Thank you both for what you have given Celina and what you have personally taught me.

Thank you, Dr. Richard Lucht, M.D. and Sergeant Detective Michael Crooke, Cumberland Police Chief and retired Indianapolis homicide detective. It's a pleasure to talk murder with you.

Hats off to my agent, Esther Scott of Wordsmith Literary Agency.

A special word of thanks to my editor Faith Black and editorial assistant Christine Hung.

Chapter One

There is something incongruous and absolutely thrilling about sipping tea while discussing murder. One has to be so careful not to say anything in bad taste. Celina smiled, her brown eyes dancing, as she instinctively scanned the February night. Early for club, she parked her Hoosier-red Sebring in front of Grace's columned mansion. The hectic guise of her business day slipped away as lawn lights cast vague shadows against the icy Geist Reservoir.

The houses of Grace's neighbors looked as frozen as the reservoir. Snow covered the fir and fruit trees as if ordered to do so by the landscaper. Six-paneled oak doors and custom-colored window blinds kept unwelcome weather in its place. Grace's house appeared sequestered as well, but welcoming rays blazed from brass candlesticks, fabricating an openness that belied secrets hiding within.

Celina felt that tremor of excitement, that slight nervousness that always accompanied these rendezvous. The dashboard clock marked ten minutes before seven. Fighting impatience, Celina leaned back against the headrest, straight, honey-blond hair falling off her high forehead and down below the shoulders. Her ivory features appeared frozen in time as she remembered the phone call from Lara that had started this secret life.

"Grace, Tamara, Romy and I are starting a new book club. Would you care to join? Wonderful! Just read Hardy's *Tess of the D'Ubervilles* and come prepared to discuss it." End of conversation. The club sounded wonderful: intimate friends, delicious food, and great literature.

"That's all I thought it was," Celina whispered to the shadows. "I had no idea this *book club* would change the tenor of my life."

Grace's mansion had been the setting for that meeting as well. The hostess poured Earl Grey tea from a china pot hand-painted with pink roses. The ladies discussed the classic for about twenty minutes. Celina remembered staring at the film of cream spreading across the dark liquid as Lara turned the conversation from ingenuous Tess to murder.

They had named themselves *The Ladies of the Club* after the book by Helen Hooven Santmyer. Outwardly, they were five ultra-conservative wives and mothers, in many ways an updated version of that respectable group of 19th century literary women: efficient, logical nurse Lara Parker with laughing eyes in an often serious face; petite, energetic Romy Kelly, who brought in extra family income by doing freelance data entry from home; soft-spoken Grace Pappas, a widowed socialite who taught kindergarten two days a week; Tamara Montgomery, who had a knack for understanding numbers; and herself, Celina Rizkallah, a corporate vice-president with a reputation for asking questions, a trait which attracted some people and greatly annoyed others.

For the sake of their children and husbands, it was important to maintain a high sense of respectability. Privately . . . well, they all agreed a woman should never consent to being less than God created her.

What would it be tonight? Robbery? Perhaps blackmail? The thought of the unknown electrified her. Tamara's phone message had divulged nothing. The urgency of an unscheduled meeting promised intrigue. No disguise was mentioned, but that, too, excluded nothing. Their most successful masquerades were generally based on allowing others to dismiss them as uninteresting. People tend not to see possibilities in someone they have already labeled as predictable.

It had been a little more difficult than usual to get away from the house tonight. Her husband had remembered that it wasn't her scheduled book club night. Fortunately, he hadn't asked any more questions when she told him Tamara had had a conflict and they needed to change the day. Tamara did have a conflict, but it probably wasn't with the date of book club. Uncomfortable with skirting the edge of truth, Celina glanced again at the clock. Close enough. It was time to go in.

Grace had recreated Southern living on the edge of Indianapolis' suburban sprawl. Reclining among the exclusive gathering of mansions called Cambridge Estates, her home accentuated the best of genteel Kentucky. The house was perfectly Grace: beautiful, elegant, laced with Southern charm.

Celina pressed the doorbell and, as was their custom on club nights, entered without waiting for it to be answered. The interior of the mansion more than kept the columned exterior's promise of unhurried refinement. High ceilings, arched doorways, and flowing lace curtains ushered guests into a world of hospitality where one expected to be served mint juleps and bread pudding with raisins soaked in bourbon and topped with Chantilly cream.

"Come in," Grace called. The club's official Southern belle looked up from her position at the cooking island. Her rich, burnished-red hair parted on the side, curved even with her chin. Centuries of ancestral French blood steeped in the Kentucky hollow of hard work and common sense had sired a slender figure with immovable moral fiber. The European aristocrats had bequeathed Grace high cheek bones, a creamy complexion, and a classic nose. Three generations of Kentuckians had handed down a slightly quirky sense of humor and a smile as wide and generous as her heart.

"I'm back here in the kitchen." Grace had a knack

for welcoming guests with a homey assurance that anything out of place in their world would soon be put right. "We're doing parent-teacher conferences this week. The first one went overtime throwing off the ones after it, so I'm a little behind schedule. Help yourself to some of those sausage balls on the buffet. There's cranberry-mustard sauce in the crystal dish."

Celina stabbed a miniature sausage ball with a toothpick, smothered it in sauce, and popped it in her mouth. "Mmm. That's delicious. I don't know which is better, the sausage ball or the sauce, but the combination is incredible. Now, what can I do to help?"

"Do you want to slice the bread or put ice in the glasses?"

"Both. Tell me about the parent-teacher conference that wrecked your schedule. Is the child struggling in class or are the parents too busy to give him attention?"

"Neither. He's probably the most academically advanced little guy in the whole kindergarten. His parents work with him at least forty-five minutes every night."

"So what's the problem?" Celina chose a serrated knife, and turning the loaf on its side, began to cut thick slices of Great Harvest bread.

"The parents are concerned that Albert doesn't have enough homework to do every day."

"In kindergarten? I didn't know kindergarteners ever had homework to do."

"If a child doesn't complete a paper in class, and it's time to move on to the next activity, I'll send it home for him to finish with his parents."

"And these parents are upset because they want their brilliant son . . . what is his name?"

"Albert."

Celina stopped slicing. "Not after Albert Einstein!"

Grace chuckled. "They didn't say. I'm hoping he was named for a beloved grandfather, but I'm afraid to ask."

"So Albert's parents are upset because he doesn't have homework to do every night?"

"Upset might be too strong a word," Grace peeled a cucumber and sliced it paper thin. "They said as concerned parents they want Albert to take school seriously and learn as much as he can in each grade. I went into a long explanation with them about how math skills are progressive, and that there is an advantage to learning them in a certain order. Both parents listened intently, then when I finished, the mother turned to the father and shaking her finger at him said, "No more algebra!"

"How did you keep a straight face?" Celina shook her head as the doorbell rang.

Within moments, Lara appeared in the kitchen pausing to wipe her wire-rimmed frames. A flurry of wet snow clung to her head, coiling her black hair into tight curls that emphasized her round face. Lara used minimal make-up, preferring the natural look of her olive complexion. Every inch genuine, she kept her nails like she kept her character: clean, unvarnished, and ready for work.

As a Cardiac Intensive Care nurse with thirteen years experience, Lara moved with a confidence which infused hope into those around her. Patients and their relatives respected her, with the occasional exception of a family member who mistook her unassuming disposition as an indication she could be ignored. One visitor who had assumed the no smoking rule didn't apply to him was on his way down in the elevator before he had time to wonder how a woman of average height and weight could move his six-foot body out of the room and down the hall with such force.

"*Whew!* The groundhog must have been right. I think we're going to have at least six more weeks of cold weather." Lara shrugged out of her heavy wool coat and hugged her friends.

"Eight, according to the Weather Channel," Romy's voice called from the hall closet where she was hanging up her coat. The fourth club member zipped into the kitchen. Romy's appearance was as tidy as her life. Stylishly short hair, the color of an acorn, required exactly eighteen minutes to go from washed to walking out the door. Five foot two, her athletic frame and toned muscles revealed strength. Her movements reminded one of quicksilver—an excess of spirit tamed for accomplishing a great work. Energized from the first flickering of her eyes each morning, she was the club fireball.

"Who ordered the meeting?" Romy asked.

"Tamara," Lara answered. "That sounds like her van pulling up in front of the house now. Let's wait until she gets in here."

"She needs a new muffler," Romy commented.

"She needs a new car," Celina amended. "It's ridiculous that Greg drives last year's Lexus while Tamara takes the children around in a vehicle with over 120,000 miles on it."

"He's an idiot," Romy shook her head in disgust. "It's too bad he doesn't just disappear."

"It would be better for the children as well as Tamara," Celina agreed.

"We could help him disappear," Romy suggested. She intended to be funny, but concern for their friend eradicated the humor.

"We're not going to do that," Grace's voice was firm.

"No, but it gives me a bit of pleasure knowing we could," Romy admitted.

The door opened, and the ladies dropped the subject as Tamara entered the room. At five foot eight, large-boned Tamara was the tallest member of their club. One-quarter Cherokee, Tamara had the naturally tanned skin of her native ancestors. Her wide eyes and open demeanor reflected an optimistic confidence in people that not even an unfaithful husband had been able to quench.

Sighing, she brushed bangs out of her eyes. The wind had played as much havoc with her auburn hair as the evening's events had meddled with her mood. A flustered expression altered her normally placid expression. "Sorry I'm late. My soon-to-be ex-husband was supposed to pick the kids up at six o'clock to take them to Chuck E. Cheese, but he didn't get to the house until six-fifty. By then the kids were hungry, not to mention grouchy and mad at me."

"Why were they mad at you?" Lara asked.

Tamara shrugged. "It's always safer to be mad at the

person you know loves you." She sighed. "Greg walked in like a hero, totally oblivious to the turmoil he had caused as the kids wondered whether or not he would show up this time. Then, when Allie couldn't find her shoes, Greg asked why I couldn't have them ready on time. Anyway, let's forget about him now." She turned to Grace, "I'm sorry I held up dinner."

"No problem. The Greek chicken is ready to take out of the oven now. Everybody grab a dish, and we'll move into the dining room."

Grace's passion for family and appreciation for beauty reflected itself in the abundance of generations-old antiques placed throughout her home, many of which represented her own Kentucky heritage. Each piece of furniture revealed a little bit of Grace's history. The old clay spittoon, no longer in use, had been an inheritance from Great Uncle Henry, who reportedly possessed the ability to make his mark straight on from ten and a half feet. Whatever the individual family members thought of chewing tobacco, they all agreed there was no denying this rare talent was a gift. The old Baptist deacon's bench had been used by an unbroken line of family members including Cousin Joe Bob who was discovered to be cooking up moonshine in the middle of a dry county. From Granny's pie safe to the embroidered linens neatly pressed and smelling faintly of dried lavender, Grace's home reflected her loves, joys, and sense of humor.

The women settled into the dining room's walnut chairs. After a short prayer thanking God for food and friendship, they began passing dishes, the tension palpable as each woman anticipated the turn in discussion. As Grace picked up her fork to take the first bite, Lara, the natural leader of the club, prompted Tamara. "Why don't you tell us about the problem?"

Tamara hesitated, her mind taking a moment to banish thoughts of her errant husband to a separate time and place. Eyes thoughtful, she debated how best to explain what she had discovered. No matter how much you believed something or how much time you had spent thinking about a concern, sharing it with another person validated it as a problem that had to be dealt with. She took a deep breath. "It has to do with my accounting work at the school's administrative office. I've been over the books countless times. School money is missing."

"How much?" Romy questioned.

"Thousands of educational dollars are disappearing from Lincoln Township accounts."

"How is that happening?" Grace asked.

"Paychecks are sent to someone who doesn't exist. The township is paying teachers who aren't real. They exist on paper—fictitious names on the salary roster. The computer issues checks to those names, and someone is cashing the checks."

"Ghost employment," Celina murmured.

"I'm sure of it. New names keep appearing on the salary list."

"Perhaps they are new teachers," Grace suggested, passing the salad around again.

"I don't know the names of all the teachers in Lincoln Township," Tamara admitted, "but some of these names I'm sure I've never heard."

"Did you check the list of teachers at our kids' school?" Lara asked. "You probably know most of the staff there."

"I thought of that. The list for Grissom Elementary is fine. Not a mistake on it. At first, I thought I must be wrong, but now I don't think so. New names are showing up too often. This is a good school system. Teachers like to work here. Turnover is low."

"Embezzlement," Lara mused.

"Not necessarily," Romy cautioned. "We don't know if the thief is inside the organization."

"As of right now, what can you prove?" Lara salted her food.

"I know the names and numbers keep changing, but I don't know who is doing it."

Romy frowned. "Can't you run a printout, and then run another one the next time they change?"

"I tried that. I highlighted the differences and showed them to Winston Dopplar. He's our senior accountant. He thinks I made the errors. The problem only showed up on the accounts I worked on. The next month everything was okay on that school's account, but a different account was off, again one I was working on. This time I took a copy to the superintendent. At least Superintendent Updike didn't act like I'm incompetent."

"Richard Updike is a very nice man," Grace agreed.

"When Alex was alive we often saw Richard and Margaret at social events. What did he say about the change in numbers?"

"He looked the numbers over in detail and asked good questions. He promised to get to the bottom of it. The next morning he was already meeting with Winston when I arrived. Winston was livid. He thought I went over his head and made him look bad."

"And Superintendent Updike?"

"Superintendent Updike thanked me for being conscientious. He said he reviewed the accounts with Winston, and that there wasn't a problem. He assured me finance is very complicated and said that I shouldn't feel bad for not understanding all of it. He's convinced only a CPA can follow the numbers."

"Patronizing," Romy scowled.

"No, it might sound that way from someone else, but not from Mr. Updike. I suspect Winston told him I couldn't understand finance."

"So, is he right?" Lara probed. "Could you be wrong?"

"No. Regardless of what they say, this is not high finance. It's just accounting. The numbers ought to add up."

"Why isn't the problem showing up on the bank balances?" Grace asked. "The account the salaries are written on should reflect the increased withdrawals."

"For one thing, the increase has been gradual. Secondly, our banking system is much more sophisticated than a checking account. We have a payroll disbursement account. The day before checks go out, the computer calculates the exact amount of each paycheck based on tax exemptions and data provided by each principal. That includes hours worked, sick days, etc. Cindy, our data processor, does that. The procedure is pretty basic. She types the information in, and then the computer tells Winston how much money is needed. Winston informs Superintendent Updike, who approves the amount. Winston orders the wire transfer. Twenty-four hours before the payroll checks are printed, I complete the process by transferring the exact amount to be paid from township investment funds to the payroll disbursement account. That way money not in use is always earning interest."

"Does this mean we're dealing with someone who is intimately acquainted with the township's payroll system?" Celina asked.

"Not necessarily. It could be someone in the Administration Office. It could even be a teller at the bank or maybe a computer hacker."

"Speaking of computer hackers, Romy, can you get into the township's bank records and check those for us?" Lara automatically began to organize. "Why don't you get copies of all transactions for the past six months?" Romy nodded, and Lara continued. "Tamara, tell us about the people in the accounting office."

"As I said, Winston Dopplar is the senior accountant. Mr. Updike thinks he's an accounting genius."

"Could he be the thief?" Lara asked.

"I don't think so. He takes too much pride in saving the system money. Saving school money is very personal with him. I hate to admit it, but he does a good job. He almost acts as if the money belongs to him."

Romy rejected the defense. "That could be a cover-up. Perhaps he thinks of it as his because he's stealing it. He might get mad when people waste resources because that leaves less money for him to steal."

"That would be nice," Tamara commented.

"Why would that be nice?" Lara asked.

"I don't like working with him," she admitted, "this would be an easy way to get rid of him."

"I don't know about easy," Lara countered before leading them to the next phase of discussion. "How can we help?"

"I need help comparing the computerized payroll ledgers with human resource personnel files showing hiring, attendance, and termination dates. Somehow I have to bring home copies of all those records, so we'll have more time to look them over. Even as an accountant, I can't devise a plausible excuse for lugging heavy payroll printouts away from the office. I can't go back to the office after hours to get them because Winston works a lot of overtime. He'll notice if they're gone."

"Is it too much information to store on a floppy disk?" Celina asked.

"A rewritable compact disc will give you enough memory," Romy answered. "Label it X-BOX 360 CHEAT CODES in case anyone sees it, Tamara. You can pretend your son created it for mine."

"Good idea," Tamara nodded.

Long after dinner ended, the women continued making plans to uncover the thief. Although this problem appeared to be simpler than ones the club had handled in the past, the ladies were meticulous in their deliberation, considering every angle.

Satisfied with their accomplishments, the ladies of the club dispersed, returning home to their husbands and children. Tamara was the last to leave. Her van pulled out of the driveway, the bass sound of her motor grumbling down the road.

The next morning Tamara sat at her desk, her grey eyes narrowing to slits as she scrutinized the suspects. Glancing back down at the figures in front of her, she used the end of her pencil to punch numbers in the calculator before shaking her head. No mistake. The numbers still didn't add up. Someone on the staff of Lincoln Township School's administration had to be stealing.

Opening her bottom desk drawer she shoved aside thick, olive-colored hanging files. She slid her hand into the side pocket of her cold leather purse, smiling as her fingers touched a CD-R. Even if seen, no one could question her taking home what looked like a list of X-Box 360 cheat codes her son had compiled and asked her to copy. "Thank you, X-box!" Popping the disc into the CD drive, she began copying files off the township server.

For two hours, Tamara's fingers flew over the keyboard retrieving payroll ledgers and resaving them on the disc until the sound of footsteps interrupted her concentration.

"What are you doing?" the senior accountant inquired.

Steeling herself to appear calm, Tamara directed her eyes to the tall, rangy man now towering over her desk. A limp strand of biscuit-brown hair fell into his eyes, adding to that gangling look teenagers usually outgrow around age seventeen. This man was twenty-eight. Chances were the look was permanent. Like a spider, she thought, all elbows and joints. "Excuse me?" she responded.

"What are you doing tonight?" Winston repeated.

"Just a quiet night at home."

"What does a single mother of four do for excitement?" Winston questioned.

Tamara stared at him, wondering if he thought that myopic look was cosmopolitan. "As a matter of fact, a quiet night at home with my kids can be pretty exciting."

"Don't you do anything else?"

She pushed her thick auburn hair off her forehead, wishing she could brush him away as easily. "Yes, I'm in a book club."

"Book club?" Cindy, the data processing clerk spoke up from her nearby desk. "Is that fun?"

Tamara hid a smile as she imagined her coworkers' shock if they knew the truth about her book club. "I enjoy it."

Chapter Two

"What type of stuff do you read?" the big-boned girl persisted, coming over to join the conversation.

"We take turns selecting the book. Last month we read *A Morbid Taste for Bones* by Ellis Peters."

"Never heard of it," Winston dismissed the book and walked back to his desk.

"One of the best mysteries ever written."

"I think it is so cool that you have a book club at your age," gushed the nineteen-year old. "How many people are in it?"

"Five women," Tamara answered, resisting an urge to point out that thirty-two was not ancient.

"How long have you been doing this?" Cindy perched on the edge of Tamara's desk, clearly avoiding work.

"Several years. We need to get back to work. How

are you coming on that data I asked you to input this morning?"

"I'm working on it," the girl avoided the question before sidetracking again. "I'm just so hungry this morning."

Tamara reached into her top drawer and pulled out half a bag of peanut M & Ms. "Here," she offered, "This should hold you over until lunch."

"Oh, no!" the data processing clerk exclaimed. "I am deathly allergic to all types of nuts." She backed up, terrified the proximity to the M & Ms would send her into anaphylactic shock. "Even if I only ate a few, I could collapse right here on the floor and die before the ambulance arrived."

"Sorry, I forgot," Tamara apologized. "I don't have anything else with me. Perhaps with all the work you have to do, the morning will go quickly." She turned back to her own work, hoping to discourage additional conversation.

The closer Tamara came to copying the last payroll ledger, the more difficult it was to concentrate. Her thoughts raced to plan her next move. Throughout the office, keyboards clicked. Roger, another accountant, chatted with the receptionist. Typically, office noises melted into the background while she worked, but this morning Tamara struggled to concentrate. Her mind felt split in half as she strained to focus on the task and remain aware of any movement towards her. One glance at the wide range of dates, and any coworker knowledgeable of township finances would question why she was making copies.

Focusing her eyes on the screen, she tried to give the impression of being totally absorbed in her work. Ninety minutes later . . . finished! All the relevant payroll information on hard drive was copied to the disc.

Now she needed to pull paper files, duplicate the originals, and then scan the copies onto disc. That was riskier. Data listing teacher starting dates and attendance was stored on the third floor.

Tamara stood, silently cautioning herself. "Slow . . . easy . . . don't draw attention to your movements." She left the open accounting area and proceeded up the front stairs. The ninety-five-year-old brick building had originally been an officer's home on Fort Benjamin Harrison before the demobilization of the finance center during the mid-nineties. Now the maze of small rooms with twelve-foot ceilings, arched doorways, original oak floors, and defunct fireplaces served as the administrative offices for the Lincoln Township School District. Tamara and the other accountants had their desks in the room a general's wife had once labeled "the finest parlor in Indiana." A private office would have been nicer, but at least they didn't have cubicles, and the windows offered an expansive view of the former parade grounds.

Entering the third floor file room, she opened several tall, gray cabinets extracting employee attendance records for half a dozen schools. Tamara went down the back staircase in hopes of avoiding coworkers.

At the second floor landing, she came face to face with the receptionist, climbing her way up. "I have been summoned," Sylvia whispered, raising her severely plucked eyebrows towards the administrative assistant's office in mock reverence.

"Flee before it's too late," Tamara whispered back, as if conspiring.

"Oh, no," Sylvia demurred, her solid body continuing up the stairs. "Never back down or she will eat you for dinner."

Tamara laughed. She enjoyed Sylvia. The woman refused to be intimidated. She was always herself. No pretense. No hedging on her birth date. Not even her hair color.

"Do you call your hair color shimmering pearl?" Cindy had once asked the down-to-earth receptionist.

"Actually, I call it gray," Sylvia replied.

Tamara smiled at the memory, but as she slid into her chair and flipped open the first file, her smile faded. The magnitude of copying teacher attendance records from all Lincoln Township schools felt overwhelming. She closed her eyes and rubbed her temple.

"Do you have a headache?" a concerned voice asked.

Tamara's eyes flew open to confront redheaded, slightly chubby Roger. She smiled. Good old Roger: hardworking, dependable, and predictable. They had worked together ever since she had been hired. At least there was one person she didn't have to worry about suspecting. His fiery hair belied an equanimous personality. For a moment Tamara considered confiding in him. The information would be so much easier to collect if they were working together. "Roger . . ." she faltered, stopping short of the revelation. "Yes. I have a headache."

"Is there anything I can do to help?" Roger glanced down at the papers on her desk. "What project are you working on? Perhaps I can help you finish it faster so you can go home early?"

"No, that's not necessary." Instinctively, Tamara flipped over the attendance records so he could not read them. Her obvious action brought a puzzled and somewhat hurt look to his eyes. Roger took a step back.

Immediately regretting her sharp tone, Tamara strove to make amends. "Thanks for offering. I'm almost done with this report. Sorry I snapped at you. This headache is so awful I can hardly think." She reached for her purse. "I'll take a couple of Excedrin."

"Is it alright if I get you some water to go with that?" he asked, wary of intruding.

Tamara nodded, grateful for a way out of the conversation. Two minutes later he was back from the break room and placing a plastic glass on her desk. "Hope this helps," he murmured before retreating.

"Thank you," she called after his back. Roger swung around and flashed a forgiving grin. Relieved, Tamara picked up the next attendance record and went to work separating employee names she knew were legitimate from those about which she had a question. She spent the rest of the morning interspersing regular job tasks with additional trips to the third floor file room.

A bustle of movement from coworkers caused Tamara to glance at her watch. Twelve o'clock. Most people generally went out for lunch. That meant faster and freer access to the attendance files.

"Nice to see you smiling again," Roger paused by her desk. "You must be feeling better."

"I am," she answered truthfully.

"I'm driving over to Wendy's. Would you like to come or is there anything I can pick up for you?"

"Yes, thank you. A chicken sandwich would be great, mayo and extra pickle," Tamara smiled, handing him a five from her purse, adding, "Nothing to drink. Is Wendy's the hot spot for everybody today?"

"It is for Sylvia, Cindy, and me. Winston was supposed to go with us, but he changed his mind. Says he has a lot of work to do. We'll be back with your order in about an hour."

"Thank you, Roger." The smile froze on Tamara's face as he walked away. "Of all people, why couldn't Winston go out to lunch today," she grumbled. Resigned to an hour of sneaking, she collected the files she wanted copied and started towards the scanner.

An office door opened, and Ms. Cole stepped out. Although barely five foot, the superintendent's administrative assistant presented an imposing figure—something in the way she carried herself. Not even her tightly permed crown of glory that, quite frankly, resembled a poodle, could detract from her aura of peremptoriness. Ms. Cole lived life in a cold, efficient manner. The only occasions when the woman appeared excited were when she thought someone was challenging Superintendent Updike. Then the poodle became a bulldog.

Attempting a cordial greeting, Tamara smiled at the administrative assistant. Ms. Cole stared at her, trying to find something to fault, before returning a curt nod and proceeding up the stairs. Oops, that was a mistake, Tamara chided herself. Smiling at Ms. Cole was definitely not normal. I wonder if she's the thief, Tamara mused, and then quickly dismissed the idea as unlikely. Amy Cole was too conventional to steal funds from Lincoln Township. It wouldn't be in character for her. On the other hand, she would blow the whistle in a second if she knew Tamara was attempting to prove school funds were being stolen. She would view Tamara's concerns as questioning the integrity of the township in general and the superintendent in particular. She would never listen to an explanation. No grace there. Ms. Cole would be in far too much of a hurry to prove her loyalty to Superintendent Updike. Not that it needed proving.

Tamara entered the converted butler's pantry now serving as a copy/shredder/scanner room. She shoved her son's CD into the CD drive connected to the computer and began scanning original papers. For the next forty minutes, Tamara worked in frustratingly slow motion, feeding one paper at a time into the machine.

"Hello, Tamara!" The voice of the senior accountant startled her into jabbing the start button twice.

"Hi, Winston!" In an effort to appear at ease, Tamara

put more enthusiasm than intended into her greeting and immediately regretted it.

Warming to the welcome, Winston entered the cramped room, his lank six-foot-four body, more than crowding the space. "What are you doing?" he asked. His pale, watery eyes peered at her from behind wire-rimmed glasses, indicating more interest in her body than in the answer to his question.

How could such a skinny person make even the smallest room feel overcrowded? Tamara wondered. "Just work," she answered, trying to find a mix between cheerful nonchalance and anything that could remotely be interpreted as encouragement. She backed up to increase the distance between them, but was rewarded with a poke in the shoulder from a wall shelf. The scanner beeped, signaling the completion of information transferred to disc. Nervous, she grabbed the papers out of the scanner and popped the disc from the CD drive.

Her feverish actions drew Winston's attention to the disc in her hands. "What kind of a disc is that?" he accused. "That doesn't look like an Office Depot CD."

"I think it's a TDK brand."

"Where did it come from?" No longer leering, Winston became the senior accountant demanding to know who was wasting company resources. "Just last month I sent out a memo stating we are only to use Office Depot brand. The township saves twenty-three-point seven-five dollars per month by buying them in bulk."

Unable to dismiss the disc as her son's when Winston had clearly observed her scanning administration information on it, Tamara improvised a new excuse. "This is an old disc I found in the back of a cabinet. It must have been bought before your memo came out. I thought I might as well use it up so as not to waste resources." To sidetrack Winston from possibly asking to see the disc, Tamara switched the topic from her to him. "That was so clever of you to arrange a bulk pricing agreement." Knowing the senior accountant to be especially fond of praise, Tamara poured it on thick. "You save the township money every time it implements one of your ideas."

Winston responded as programmed. Looking like a pompous giraffe, he bragged, "If they paid me just twenty percent of what I save them with my ideas, I could be a rich man in no time. I've thought about doing that for companies on a consulting basis," he confided.

"I'm sure you could," Tamara agreed, trying to end the conversation.

"I already make enough money to take a woman out and treat her right," he hinted.

"Mr. Dopplar," Ms. Cole's crisp voice spoke from the hallway. "Superintendent Updike would like to see you."

Winston grudgingly followed the administrative assistant, leaving Tamara to heave a sigh of relief as she shoved the disc into the manila folder she was carrying.

By 4:30 that afternoon, Tamara was more than ready for the workday to end. She was anxious to see her kids and hear about school. She questioned whether or not she should have sent Allie to school, even though the child didn't have a fever. The five-year old had spent an hour proclaiming she was sick. Tamara wondered how Keith's report on the leopard had gone and if Debbie had passed her math test. Julie was the only one of her children about whom she did not worry. Giggly, care-free Julie seemed to live a charmed life, oblivious to the challenges and inconveniences the rest of the world en-countered.

"Ms. Montgomery," a peremptory voice demanded behind her. Ms. Cole had the timing of a sniper. One never knew when to expect a hit. "Did you generate the monthly payroll distribution report?"

"Yes, it's right here." Relieved it was work she had already completed, Tamara picked the file up off her desk and handed it over.

A second floor office door opened and the boss came down the steps. A shade under six feet, he was a man of notable, but not intimidating stature. Threads of silver highlighted his brown hair. Richard Updike was a man for whom life worked well. Born with the natural diplomacy of a politician and the enthusiasm of a car salesman, he was a leader teachers and admin-istrators worked overtime to please. Good things came to him so often, he expected success. He was rarely disappointed.

"Superintendent Updike!" Ms. Cole's voice soft-ened, almost acquiring a submissive tone. "Here is the payroll distribution report I promised you."

The superintendent beamed. "Great! Thank you both for your hard work. Amy, do you have a minute to go over the projected enrollment figures for next year?" Mr. Updike and his faithful poodle disappeared up the stairs, and Tamara relaxed.

The telephone on her desk rang. Her estranged husband's irritatingly smooth voice responded to her greeting. "Tamara, I'm calling to let you know I'll be picking the children up at 5 o'clock instead of 6 o'clock."

"If you pick them up at 5 o'clock, that won't give them enough time to do their homework."

"I have tickets for the Pacers game," he steamrolled her. "I already called the kids and told them. They're excited."

"You called the kids without talking to me first?"

"I don't need your permission to talk to my kids."

"It's not about permission. It's about checking schedules. They need to be in bed at a decent hour on school nights."

"You're always trying to control everyone and everything. That's what broke up our marriage."

"I thought it was that little redheaded receptionist that broke up our marriage," Tamara retorted. "Or was it the blond customer service representative? Anyway we were discussing what schedule would be in the best interest of the children."

"It is in the best interest of the children to spend time with their father. That's why Indiana courts mandate one night of visitation per week in addition to alternating weekends and holidays."

"Bonehead," Tamara muttered under her breath. "I

don't believe the court's intention was for them to not get their homework done. Debbie has a science test tomorrow."

"You know tonight is my night with the kids. Obviously, you should have planned ahead. Stop saving all their work for when they're supposed to be with me."

Tamara could hear the spite in his voice. She knew he was intentionally putting her on the defensive, but still couldn't stop herself from rising to the bait. "I'm not saving their work! They study every night."

"You get the kids all the time and then you try to control what they do when they're with me."

"This isn't about control. It's about parenting." Tamara insisted.

"I'm picking them up at 5 o'clock. You have no choice."

Tamara knew that tone as well as the children did. No negotiation. No compromise. The court was on his side. "What time will you have them home?"

"We'll get dinner first. Game starts at seven-thirty and should be over by ten-thirty. I'll have them back by eleven o'clock or eleven-thirty."

"How can they possibly get up for school tomorrow if they go to bed so late?" she tried one more time.

He ignored the question. "Sometimes I think it would be great to have my kids permanently back home in their real house, not that Cracker Jack box where you're living. They would be better off, and you could be the one getting leftover time."

She knew he didn't mean it. She knew having the

children would interfere with his social life, and he would not tolerate having to adjust his schedule for anyone. Still, the moment he started insinuating a custody battle, she backed off. "Try to get them in as early as possible."

"They'll be back when I bring them," he snapped and hung up.

Movement on the staircase caused Tamara to look up and see the superintendent coming down in a navy Burberry overcoat. "Good night," he smiled and was gone.

Four-forty. Almost time to go home. Tamara organized her desk and pulled her purse out of the lower file drawer. Pleased with her day's work, she reached for the folder where she had hidden the disc labeled X-BOX 360 CODES. It wasn't there. Startled, she scoured her desk again. Think, she instructed herself, think. You were standing in the copy room. It finished scanning. Winston saw the disc and made a fuss about the brand name. You told him it was an old one and stuffed it in the folder. Which folder was that? Alarm turned to panic as she remembered. It was the file containing the payroll distribution report, the folder she had so agreeably turned in to Ms. Cole, who had then handed it over to the superintendent.

Tamara slumped down in her chair. Not only had she failed to gather additional information, but now she had jeopardized her own career. She had created a disc that undoubtedly proved accounting discrepancies and contained personal employee information that shouldn't be seen outside of Human Resources. She couldn't have implicated herself more if she had confessed to stealing the money. She had intended the disc to be used as evidence. Now it would be—against her. What were the three things a prosecutor had to prove? Means? Yes, transferring funds in and out of township accounts was part of her regular job responsibility. Motive? A single mother of four was practically the definition of needing money. Opportunity? Every day right from her own desk. I even sound guilty to me, she thought.

Tamara's thoughts raced. Even if the disc evidence is so circumstantial they can't convict me, I will still look guilty. My personal and professional credibility will be destroyed. How will I support my kids without a job? Greg might really go for custody then. With his money and high-priced lawyers that wouldn't be difficult if I gave any cause at all.

I can't let this happen, Tamara determined. Superintendent Updike already left so he won't be in his office. I'll sneak in and get it back. He doesn't know the disc exists, so he won't notice when it's gone. She grabbed a file folder and started up the front stairs. Her hand barely touched the knob on his office door when a glacial voice demanded, "What do you think you're doing?"

Tamara turned to face her accuser. "I made a mistake on the payroll distribution report. I wanted to get it back and fix it."

"You made a mistake." Contempt shot from Ms. Cole's face.

"Yes, and I want to correct it."

"It's too late," the administrative assistant pronounced as if eternal salvation was no longer an option. "The superintendent took the report home with him to review it."

"He took it home," Tamara repeated horrified.

"Yes. He will see your error. And if he doesn't, I will make sure he knows first thing tomorrow morning."

Stunned, Tamara turned and walked down the back stairs without responding. There had to be a way to get that disc back before he saw it. Immediately her thoughts turned to the club. Lara will be able to devise a plan. Again, Tamara hesitated. She hated to admit her failure. Failure was a kind word. This fiasco had been pure stupidity and that was one thing for which club members gave no grace. As loyal and loving as the group could be, they spared no words when it came to accountability for actions, especially within their own circle. Tamara's thoughts reverted to the information on the disc. If Mr. Updike saw those files, the whole mess would come to light and they would know anyway.

Her sense of self-preservation greater than her embarrassment, Tamara avoided the crowded accountant area and walked to the pay phone located in the hall. One eye on the empty hallway, she began to dial.

"Pappas residence," a Southern voice drawled.

"Grace, this is Tamara. I don't have a lot of time to talk. Club needs to meet tonight." Tamara recounted losing the disc. "I could lose my job, maybe even custody of my kids."

"We won't allow that to happen," Grace soothed. "Let's meet here at seven-thirty."

"I'll tell the others." Tamara clicked the receiver. Depositing another thirty-five cents, she dialed the next number as Sylvia and Roger entered the hallway.

"Come on, Romy, answer," Tamara urged, turning away as the receptionist and accountant neared. On the first ring, the call went to voice mail. She must be online. "Romy, it's Tamara. Just a reminder book club is at Grace's. Very important discussion. We need everyone to be there so we can . . . uh . . . talk about the social impact and . . . style of writing. Seven-thirty tonight. Thanks." Tamara hung up knowing how awkward her sentences had sounded. She waited until Sylvia and Roger left the hall before dialing the third number.

"Americas Group," answered a receptionist's cheerful voice. "How may I direct your call?"

"Celina Rizkallah, please."

"One moment, please. I'll connect you."

Tamara impatiently drummed her fingers on top of the pay phone, hoping she wouldn't hear the obnoxious tones of voice mail.

"Hi. You've reached the office of Celina Rizkallah, Vice President of Training and Development. I'm away from my desk or on another line. Please leave a message, and I'll be glad to return your call."

"Celina, this is Tamara. Club meeting. Be at Grace's by seven-thirty tonight."

Next call. "Midwest Memorial Medical Center," a volunteer answered.

"Cardiac Intensive Care Unit, please."

The line clicked, and a female voice identified herself, "Cardiac Intensive Care Unit. Nurse Parker speaking."

"Lara!" Tamara recounted the events leading up to the loss of the disc going into more detail than she had on any of the other calls. "I need to get it back before the superintendent realizes what he has."

"It doesn't sound like there's much of a choice. We'll go get the disc tonight. Hopefully, he won't have already seen it. Have you contacted the other members of the club?"

"We're meeting at the mansion at seven-thirty."

"I'll be there with a plan." The intercom system announced a code blue in the background. "Gotta go. Patient just went into cardiac arrest." The line went dead.

Tamara hung up the phone feeling a momentary reprieve before the sound of squeaking tennis shoes rubbed the relief out. She swung around. Winston stood beside the cooler, drinking his water, silently watching. Tamara shivered, and hurried back to her computer.

Chapter Three

Lara formulated a plan while moving between patients. She finished her shift, and then detoured past the Updike mansion on her way home. It took several calls on her cell phone before she finally found someone who knew the information she wanted. Next, she called each club member, explaining the role she was to play, and instructing her to bring items for tea. Finally, she went home and changed into her favorite church dress.

Synchronized to the minute when the situation demanded it, all four cars pulled up outside of Grace's house within thirty seconds of each other. Inside, anticipation gave way to a cool marshalling of their resources. Although each member privately thought Tamara had been careless to allow the disc out of her possession, they united in closing ranks to protect one of their own.

Lara mapped out the plan, instructing each woman on the part she was about to play. Roles understood, the club members moved silently, single file back under the anonymous cloak of darkness.

The white Odyssey slid through the night, carrying five well-dressed women and a cargo of innocent looking, heavy-duty cardboard boxes. A sharp gust of wind whipped through the air, causing the van to mimic the internal shaking they felt.

"Are you sure no one will be home tonight?" Tamara's question broke the silence. "Yes, ma'am," Grace answered. "I called the superintendent's wife and told her I had four extra tickets to the off-Broadway production of *The Lion King*. That was the only thing I could think of to get them all out of the house and not leave the children home with a baby sitter. Plus, those tickets are hard to get. I thought she would be willing to rearrange their schedule. Fortunately, they hadn't already seen the play."

"Where's Elena?"

"She's spending the night with my parents," Grace explained. Dad will drive her to school in the morning. They are always so excited to have her; they never ask why."

The evening returned to silence. This was the first time they had ever actually broken into a house. Usually, they impersonated someone to get in while the owners were there. "For the record," Grace commented, "I am not happy 'breaking and entering.' I think this is far different than pretending to be someone and being invited inside the house."

"We don't have time to wait for an invitation, not even one that's contrived," Lara responded. "Plus, the house is too big. "We'd never get the whole place searched without it being empty. It must be fourteen thousand square feet."

"Seventeen thousand," Romy corrected. The little but mighty member ran her life on a system. Color swatches coordinated her wardrobe. She bought groceries on Mondays so she could get triple value for her coupons. Thursday was etched in stone as cleaning day. As far as any other activity, if it wasn't on the calendar, it didn't happen. She could account for every nickel spent on a gumball, and the bank account *always* balanced. If Congress allocated the nation's finances with the same resourcefulness and skill Romy ran her household budget, there would be no national debt.

Loyalty induced the only exception to her methodical lifestyle. When the ladies called, this faithful friend answered. The club was Romy's one rebellion to a well-ordered existence.

"Besides," Romy continued, feeling no qualms about what she viewed as a necessary visit, "it's not really 'breaking and entering.' I'll get us in without breaking a thing." When that explanation was met with disgusted silence, she tried again, "It's not even a stranger's house. You know the Updikes, Grace. If they knew you wanted to visit, I'm sure they would invite you."

"I'm sure they would make it for a time they were home too," Grace retorted.

"That wouldn't work very well for our purposes."

Lara intervened. The van continued past Ashford Point to a place where houses were farther apart and the trees closer together. Each of the five ladies sat alone with her thoughts.

Lara tightened her grip on the steering wheel, resisting an urge to speed the night to completion. She would have rather been home overseeing John's math homework and reviewing Kelsey's social studies report. The whole reason she worked part time was to limit her hours and be available for her family. Now, here she was on a school night, out on the road while her husband and children stayed home.

Although she said nothing, Lara privately wondered if perhaps Grace was right, and the break-in was crossing a line none of them really wanted to cross. Unfortunately, no one could think of a more effective plan, and they did have to help Tamara out of this mess. Her eight-year old, John, would call it their club code of honor if he knew about it. The five club members were similar to sisters, even closer in some ways, since they had chosen to be part of that circle. No matter what mess one of the ladies got herself into and no matter how much of it was her own fault, they were still *obligated* to help. Obligated sounded like they didn't want to help and, well, tonight she guessed they didn't. Except for Romy. Romy seemed to be enjoying tonight a little too much.

A sudden gale threw a handful of snow into the van's path. Pushing resentment aside, Lara turned her attention back to the road. She definitely did not want to have an accident and be required to explain her presence on 113th Street tonight. Lara glanced over at Grace in the front passenger's seat. Only manicured hands clutching and re-clutching her "Teachers Have Class" book bag betrayed her nervousness.

Each woman gave her mind over to the part she was to play; each wondering if she would be able to perform to the degree required for success. Tonight was different from previous scams. In the past they had used their various talents in ways that, while not quite straightforward, only dabbled in the illegal.

Celina mentally reviewed their individual skills. Lara's leadership and consistency in following clues to their logical conclusion; Romy's computer hacking abilities, although the club preferred to say she had a talent for accumulating technical information; Grace, who, between her career as a beloved kindergarten teacher and her status as a widowed socialite, always knew someone who knew someone who knew the information they needed to know (and most importantly was willing to share); and Tamara's mathematical aptitude as a numbers cruncher. Unfortunately, Celina reflected, her own brief stint as a Speech and Theatre major in college seemed to come closest to filling the need of the night. If this all depends on me, we could really be in trouble, she brooded.

Signaling briefly, Lara turned the van down a long paved driveway, screened by double rows of fir trees. One of the cardboard boxes stuffed beneath the seats slid forward, nudging hosed legs out of their way.

Romy's swift kick sent it back under the seat. The van bumped over the narrow bridge, passing a regulation tennis court on the left and a private fishing pond on the right. Geist Reservoir gleamed through oak trees in the backyard. Empty docks waited for spring and the return of the family sailboat, pontoon, and jet skis. Carbon black against the sulfur night, the mansion painted a shadowed tableau across the sky.

The van pulled up to the side door, rolling to a reluctant stop. One by one, the ladies stepped onto the snow-blown pavement. Outside the manufactured warmth of the van, the night seemed to hold itself in suspense, as if understanding it was merely backdrop for a bit of theater about to unfold. The elegantly coiffed ladies lugged cardboard boxes and stepped carefully over patches of ice to congregate near the side door and shake snow off their high heels.

"According to this security company's procedure, once we open the door we have ninety seconds before the alarm goes off," Lara began. "The alarm is connected to a live guard via computer."

"That's the way it is at work too," Tamara nodded. "Our security, fire and sump pump alarm are connected through the computer."

Lara continued her explanation. "If we don't call in the password for a false alarm within ninety seconds, a patrol car is notified to check it out. Those are off-duty police officers working a second job. An officer is guaranteed to be here within five minutes, maybe even three."

"How do you know this?" Grace demanded.

"All these security companies post little signs on the front lawn warning intruders that the house is protected. After work, I drove by here. The sign in the Updike's yard says PROTECTED BY MIDWEST SECURITY COMPANY. I called several friends, told them we were considering a security system, and asked about theirs. Eventually, I hit someone who uses Midwest Security Company. She told me their procedures. Does everyone know what to do? Alright then, let's do it."

Romy snapped open a thin gunmetal tool box and stepped under the porch light. Pulling out a slender strip of steel and a small hairpin-like tool, she went to work on the double lock.

"I thought you were going to use a credit card or something." Grace's shocked voice whispered. "Where did you learn that?"

"From an old boyfriend." Romy whispered, her chin length, acorn-colored hair swinging in time to her quick movements. "Credit cards don't work for this type of lock."

"An old boyfriend?"

"Well, she did grow up in Milwaukee," Celina said.

"I think your mom let you hang out with the wrong people," Grace disapproved.

"Now *we're* the wrong people," Celina giggled.

"That's okay. I'll never tell Mom," Romy promised. The door gave a grunt. A lock popped. A little more work by Romy and the dead bolt groaned open. "Ha!" Romy exclaimed, examining the lock, "not a scratch on the striker plate." They hurried inside, leaving the back door slightly ajar.

Without another word, the ladies went to work. Lara walked through the house flipping on kitchen, hall, and living room lights before heading upstairs to turn on a bedroom lamp. Pulling a shiny steel teakettle out of her box, Tamara put water on to boil. Grace spread a crisp linen cloth over the living room coffee table. Romy extracted cucumber and watercress sandwiches from one of the cardboard boxes and a silver platter from another. Celina placed napoleons, cream puffs, and strawberries dipped in chocolate on a three-tiered serving dish.

Suddenly, a piercing high tone split the calm. An amplified voice announced to the house, "Burglary! Burglary! You are entering a secured area. Leave immediately! Burglary! Burglary!" The voice stopped, and the screeching alarm resumed.

"Keep working, ladies!" Lara admonished. "Security is on its way."

The alarm continued to announce their presence, alternating a siren with authoritative commands to leave. Outside, a blue light bolted to the northwest corner of the garage flashed, identifying the specific house requiring a security check. The ladies moved faster. Lara placed five copies of *The Hound of the Baskervilles* around the family room before opening the flue and lighting a gas fire. A scream from the teapot announced water had reached a rolling boil. Tamara moved to fill china cups.

Romy pulled out a platter of ribbon sandwiches and pastry cornucopias filled with Italian chicken salad out of the box. "Good grief, Celina," she exclaimed. "Look at all this food. You overdid it."

"She always makes things too complicated for herself," Tamara agreed, dumping warm sausage rolls encased in puff pastry onto individual plates.

"Could we discuss my personal neuroses some other time?" Celina retorted, setting crystal jars of whipping cream and homemade strawberry jelly next to the silverware. "Right now let's just get this tea party ready."

"Sixty seconds," Lara announced, picking up a tray of plates and silverware. Celina stuffed the cardboard boxes into the bottom of the kitchen pantry. Focus shifted to the formal living room. Grace opened her bookbag. Pulling out her own family pictures, she placed them around the room. Lara stripped a large family portrait from the wall, sliding it under the sofa before replacing it with an artist's rendering of Grace. Romy dashed up the stairs to place an 8 × 10 of Grace beside the master bed.

Tamara distributed embroidered linen napkins, and then stood by the bay window watching for security. "They're here," she announced, as a silver Crown Victoria with MIDWEST SECURITY COMPANY written on the side pulled into the drive.

Romy hurried down the stairs and into a formal living room that looked like something out of *House and Garden*. She settled on to one of the two Bradford sofas and examined the main stage of their drama. Rich Oriental rugs covered thick, lush carpeting. A grand piano and an old-fashioned secretary's desk filled the room without dwarfing it. An antique Silver Cross carriage provided a beautiful accent. Could they pull off this hoax? Nervous, Romy stuffed a sausage roll into her mouth. Maybe Celina did know what she was doing when she brought loads of food.

Grace walked to the front door as the others took their places in the living room. At the sound of doorbell chimes, she counted to five and flung open the carved oak door. Two policemen moonlighting as neighborhood security stood there.

"I'm so glad you're here, officers," Grace's Southern charm oozed out in extra syllables, her personal reservations to the evening's plan dissipating in club loyalty.

The officers stepped under the hallway's pearl chandelier, their eyes sweeping the house for anything unusual. The tall, lanky officer greeted her. "Good evening, ma'am. I'm Detective Crooke. This is my partner, Detective Hubbard." He indicated a shorter, pudgy man smiling behind him. "Are you the homeowner?"

"Yes, I'm Margaret Updike. The alarm has gone crazy, and I can't shut it off. Can you help?"

"Yes, ma'am. Where is your master control?"

"Through here." Grace led Detective Crooke out of sight as the alarm continued to protest intruders. In less than a minute, the obnoxious sound cut off in mid accusation, leaving the listeners with, "Burglary! Burglary! You are—" Celina bit her lip to crush a smile.

Unsure what to do next, the ladies sat there. From

their vantage point in the living room, they could see Officer Hubbard beginning his search of the hallway. Romy bit into a napoleon, and Celina brushed imaginary crumbs off her lap while they waited for him to notice their presence.

Officer Hubbard opened the entryway coat closet and peered inside—clearly nothing of interest. Still without noticing them, he stepped across the hallway and slid his arm along the wall until his fingers felt a switch. Electric candles from a crystal chandelier flooded the satin wallpapered room and revealed a mahogany table with seating for twelve. A tall silver urn filled with silk flowers the colors of jewels gleamed in the light.

He flicked the lights off and stepped back across the hall toward them. The moment his eyes lit on them, he stopped, taking in the scene of four ladies, dressed as if for church, primly sipping tea while they stared at him in silence.

The officer smoothed back hair that was more memory than follicle. "Ladies," he nodded. Then, looking as guilty as if he had just interrupted a meeting of the Women's Missionary Union, the officer nodded again and disappeared down the hall.

They waited. Romy tried not to bounce her foot against the sofa's wood frame. Lara readjusted her glasses, apprehensive she might see something she hadn't accounted for in her plan. Tamara appeared jittery, half expecting Ms. Cole to appear and accuse her of vilifying the superintendent. Only Celina remained calm, more eager to know what was going on than she was disturbed by the possibilities of what could happen next.

After several minutes, the sound of footsteps on hardwood floors announced the return of Grace and the policemen. This time, Grace introduced the men.

"Ladies, this is Detective Crooke and his partner . . ." Grace paused.

"Detective Tim Hubbard, ma'am," the shorter man offered reappearing behind.

"Detective?" Celina spoke up. "For home security?"

"This is part time, ma'am," Detective Hubbard explained with a good-natured smile. "Our day job is homicide."

"What caused the alarm?" Lara prompted the conversation in the direction that would get the detectives out the door the fastest.

"The back door must not have been completely closed. Evidently the wind blew it open and set the alarm off." Grace turned to the officers. "This is my book club night. My husband is away on business, and the children are at their grandmother's house. I was a little bit afraid with it being only women in the house. You hear such strange things on the news. I set the alarm after my friends arrived. I'm so sorry to have bothered you for nothing."

"No problem, ma'am. Setting the alarm was a good idea," Detective Crooke reassured her. "We'll take a closer look around the place to make sure nothing is out of order. May I see your identification?"

Grace's eyes moved to her friends sipping tea as if she wondered why someone else would be giving a tea party in her home.

"Just standard procedure," he added.

"Certainly," she smiled. "I appreciate your carefulness. Will my driver's license do?"

"Yes, ma'am. That'll be fine."

"I'll run upstairs and get it." Grace turned toward the tapestry-covered stairs. Halfway up, she paused with one hand on the curved oaken banister as if just remembering. "Oh, I forgot. Nordstrom's called me. I left my license in the shoe department this afternoon when I wrote a check. I have to go pick it up tomorrow."

The detective's posture stiffened, so slightly the difference was felt more than seen. He eyed the hostess warily, plainly not believing Grace was telling the truth, but unsure why she would lie to him. "Do you have any other form of identification?" he asked.

Right on cue, Celina spoke up. "What about her picture?" She pointed to the professional sketch hanging on the wall.

"Here's one of the whole family." Lara motioned toward an enlarged snapshot taken of Grace's entire extended family, including second and third cousins. The ladies had thought that would be safer than a formal portrait of the immediate family. It was possible the security officers had met Superintendent Updike at a school event or seen his picture in the paper. It was unlikely he would 'Where's Waldo' through all sixty-four of Grace's relatives to look for a familiar face.

"Nice sketch," Detective Crooke nodded appreciatively at the wall. "Hubbard, why don't you start in the kitchen? I'll check out the upstairs."

Detective Hubbard grunted agreement. Grace followed.

The kitchen was immaculate. Counters clear, the steel chrome of a Moen faucet gleamed, not a measuring spoon out of place. Detective Hubbard opened the pantry. The empty cardboard boxes the ladies had brought their props in were stuffed haphazardly beneath the orderly shelves of breakfast cereal and cans of vegetables. Surprised by the contrast, Detective Hubbard glanced at Grace.

"Oh, now you know my housecleaning secrets," Grace confessed. "Don't tell my guests."

Hubbard's round face broke into a grin. "My wife does the same thing when company's coming. Everything looks clear in here. I'll check out the basement. Is this the door?"

Grace felt a sudden panic as she realized she had no idea which door led downstairs. Without waiting for an answer, he pulled it open. Fortunately, the officer had chosen the logical door directly beneath the main staircase. He flipped on a switch and disappeared down the steps.

"Ma'am," Detective Crooke reappeared, "Everything's clear upstairs. Once Detective Hubbard is finished downstairs, we'll leave you and your friends to get back to your book. *The Hound of the Baskervilles,* is it?" He smiled. "I noticed several copies on the coffee table. I love a good mystery. Conan Doyle is one of my favorites." The sound of pool balls smashing drew him to the top of the basement stairs "Ready to go, Tim?" he prompted.

A sheepish Detective Hubbard appeared at the doorway. "Nice pool table!"

"Thank you," Grace smiled, stopping just short of her usual, 'you'll have to come by and play some time.' "And I appreciate you checking the house out." She walked the officers back to the main hallway.

"Our pleasure, ma'am," Detective Crooke assured her. "Glad to see it was just the wind blowing the back door open." He paused in front of the living room where the club sat waiting. "Ladies, enjoy your book discussion."

"Would you like some cookies or sandwiches to take with you?" Celina offered.

"No, thanks," Detective Crooke smiled.

"Maybe just one," Detective Hubbard contradicted, accepting the two she offered.

The carved oak door shut securely behind the policemen. Grace bolted the door and leaned against it, exhausted by the pretense. Romy immediately turned to attack Celina. "Would you like some cookies or sandwiches to take with you?" she mimicked. "What on earth were you thinking?"

"It was the polite thing to do," Celina defended herself. "We were all eating."

"It looked suspicious. Nobody gives the security guards something to eat. It's like offering something to your heating and air conditioning man when he comes for the yearly service check."

"I always offer repairmen a Coke or cup of coffee."

"And they charge you for the time it takes to drink it too."

"They probably will remember you," Lara said, "but they're gone now. Let's get this job done."

"I certainly feel safe after seeing how quickly someone can break into a home with double locks and an alarm system," Grace announced. "I thought my home was protected from burglars, but seeing what we did here, I'm not sure anymore."

"Anyone can break into your home if they really want to get in," Romy assured her.

"Anyone?"

"Well, I can." Romy verified. "All I have to know is what deterrents you have so I can decide how to circumvent them. You see . . ."

"That's okay," Grace interrupted. "You don't have to tell me. I prefer to live with some of my fantasies. I especially don't need to hear more about how you know these things. Some things not even a best friend should know."

"This place is huge," Celina complained, looking around. "It's more than twice as big as Grace's place. We'll be here all night searching these rooms."

"We don't have all night!" Tamara protested, opening the drawer of a Queen Anne coffee table. She pushed it back in. Nothing but painted marble coasters that looked like miniature Rembrandts.

"We're looking for an office report. It's not going to be in the formal living room," Lara stated. "Think this through logically. He is not trying to hide the disc from us. He doesn't even know we're looking for it. He may not even know he has it. That disc is either going to be in his briefcase or on his desk where he can look at it, someplace where he would use it. Those are the rooms where we need to look."

"You're right," Tamara agreed. "I'll find the family room. Pray he didn't see the disc before they left for *The Lion King*."

Romy opened a paneled closet door in the hallway. "No briefcase here."

"His bedroom is another possibility. It's probably on the second floor." Lara started up the stairs.

"I'll come with you," Grace offered.

"They may have another sitting area downstairs. I'll check out the basement," Celina announced.

After leaving the family room, Tamara migrated to the superintendent's study. A brass Tiffany desk lamp lighted the room, throwing shadows to the corners. Floor to ceiling custom built bookshelves lined three walls. A massive antique mahogany desk took center stage. A matching work table stood perpendicular, forming an L shape, and holding his computer and a CD file.

Tamara started with the CD file, searching through the files one by one but without finding anything. She reached across the desk to turn off the brass reading lamp when her eyes caught the soft gleam of superior leather under the desk. Tamara snapped the briefcase open. It took less than ten seconds to find the folder containing her report and a disc. "X-Box 360 Codes" was handwritten across the label. Had he viewed it or not? No way to tell.

"I found the disc," she announced in the hallway.

"Good! Let's get our stuff and get out of here," Lara said.

Grace's burnished red head popped around the corner of a room. "You found it?"

"That's all we need," Romy affirmed. "Let's get this place cleaned up."

Suddenly, a scream shriller than the alarm split the night, followed by a sobbing, hysterical, "He's dead!"

Celina! The four friends darted down the stairs, hampering each other in a race to her aid. They followed the sound of heaving sobs through the media center and exercise room to find Celina several feet away from an open closet door. Tumbled at her feet lay a man's body, an ice pick protruding from just below his breast bone.

Chapter Four

"**A**re you alright?" Grace slipped her slender arm around Celina's shaking shoulders.

"I just opened the door, and he fell out," Celina protested, denying any involvement with the body at her feet.

"He's dead," Lara pronounced, kneeling beside the corpse to check for a pulse. "Not much blood. I wonder who the man was?"

"Winston." In a small, stunned voice Tamara spoke for the first time since seeing the body. "Winston Dopplar, the senior accountant."

"This doesn't make sense. Why didn't Detective Hubbard find the body when he checked out the basement?" Romy interrupted.

"He must not have checked all the closets," Tamara offered.

"I didn't get the impression he was quite as thorough as Detective Crooke," Lara agreed. "I think he was more interested in the pool table."

"Can you imagine what would have happened if he had found us here with Winston's dead body?" Tamara shuddered.

"We've got to get out of here," Romy urged.

"What are we going to do with this body?" Grace questioned.

"We're just going to shove him right back into that closet and leave him there," Romy answered.

"Without getting help?" Grace protested.

Celina took a deep breath as her sense of self preservation kicked in. "He's beyond help. Plus, we can't very well call and report the body. Excuse me, detectives, do you mind coming back? It seems there was a break-in. In fact, it was us. As long as you're here, you might as well take a look at that dead body we found in the basement. Ladies, we need to walk out that door right now."

"And leave my fingerprints all over his body!" Lara glared at her. "I felt for a pulse. I checked for a heartbeat."

Celina marched over to the snack bar. Pulling the wrist of her sleeve down over her fingers, she used the wool as a barrier to open drawers without her skin touching the handles. Finally, she found a washcloth. Using the cloth to turn the tap water on, she wet the cloth before marching back to the dead Winston. Avoiding looking at the ice pick, she began scrubbing the places on his body Lara had touched.

"Will that work?" Romy asked.

"I don't know," Celina admitted.

"What else did you touch, Celina?" Lara questioned.

"Just the door knob, not any part of him." Celina responded scrubbing the brass handle.

"Here. Hand me that washcloth," Lara demanded. Celina handed it to her. Using the cloth to pull his head backward, Lara maneuvered the upper portion of the body backward into the closet. "He doesn't look like he's been dead very long," she observed. "He's not very stiff."

"Now, what about the rest of him?" Romy questioned. "How are we going to get that bony body back into the closet without touching him?"

Lara pinched one pant leg with the cloth and lifted it backward. It dropped before she could get it all the way into the closet. After several tries and with assistance from her friends, the sprawled body of the dead senior accountant rested uncomfortably within the doorframe. Tamara slammed the door. "Let's get out of here."

Celina tucked the incriminating washcloth into her skirt waistband to take home and throw away. All five of the women flew up the stairs. Tamara and Celina tossed the uneaten food into one of the empty cardboard boxes. Dirty plates went in next. Lara replaced the pictures of the Updike family in the living room and grabbed the five copies of this month's book. Romy ran upstairs to collect the pictures of Grace and turn off the lights.

"I brought cleaner and paper towels for wiping the counters," Lara announced. "Use them thoroughly. We especially don't want any traces of our having been here now."

"Why didn't one of us think to wear our gloves?" Celina moaned.

"Because it never occurred to us that we would find a dead body, and the police would be scouring the place for fingerprints," Romy retorted.

Counters wiped. Lights off, they were ready to leave. "Wait! We don't know the code to reset the alarm!" Tamara panicked.

"Wash the alarm pad in case it has Grace's fingerprints on it. If they notice it isn't on, they'll think they forgot to set it," Lara said. Tamara didn't believe that but had reached the point of not caring. Her only priority was to get out of the house safely. She patted her pocket to make sure the disc was still there.

Two minutes later, the ladies of the club left the Updike mansion. But Winston stayed quietly behind.

"Tamara Montgomery, call on line two," the receptionist announced.

"Thank you, Sylvia." Heart pumping, Tamara picked up the receiver expecting the police.

"Tamara, it's Lara. What's happening there?"

"Business as usual."

"What do you mean? Haven't they announced Winston's death?"

"Not a word." Tamara carefully phrased her next sentence. "We're a little bit shorthanded today. Our senior accountant called in sick. He's taking a few days off."

"A few days!" Lara exclaimed. "The man's dead! He's taking forever off!"

"Not that I've heard," Tamara responded.

"What! Were you wrong? Is the dead man someone other than Winston?"

"Ah, no. That was accurate information."

"It was Winston?" Lara verified.

"Most definitely."

"Tamara, I know that man was dead."

Frustrated, Tamara struggled to communicate without revealing the topic in front of coworkers. "I don't doubt that."

"But he called in sick?"

"So I've been told."

"By who?" Lara questioned.

"Yes, Superintendent Updike is certainly in favor of keeping the salaries of Lincoln Township teachers at a competitive level."

"Superintendent Updike claims Winston called in sick?"

"Yes!" Tamara sighed with relief at being understood.

"If he said Winston would be out for a few days, then he knows he's not coming back right away," Lara reasoned.

"Exactly!"

"What are we going to do about that?"

"I haven't a clue," Tamara admitted, suddenly noticing Ms. Cole standing in the aisle staring at her. Hurrying to end the conversation, Tamara concluded. "Mr. Updike is an extremely intelligent man. He is certainly the Indiana superintendent to watch. Thank you so much for calling. He appreciates the support of the community."

Dropping the phone back into its cradle, Tamara smiled at the superintendent's administrative assistant.

"Who was that call from?" Ms. Cole questioned, coming closer.

"A parent wanting to say she thinks Superintendent Updike is doing a fine job."

"Who are her children?"

"Jessica and Jeffrey," Tamara threw out two common names.

"I meant their last names," Ms. Cole's icy tone constituted a verbal reprimand.

"I think it began with a S."

She frowned at Tamara's incompetence. "What school do the children attend?"

"Lincoln High South."

"Grades?"

"Freshman and junior." At that moment Tamara felt as if she were in second grade.

"What exactly did she say about Superintendent Updike?"

Tamara refrained from retorting that the caller was interested in the dead body in Mr. Updike's basement. "She was glad to hear Mr. Updike secured the federal grant providing raises for the teachers."

"That was only for elementary staff. Why would she care if her children are in high school?"

"She . . . has a little one starting kindergarten next year," Tamara invented.

"Next year she'll have a senior, a sophomore, and a kindergartner? How odd!"

Tamara shrugged her shoulders slightly in lieu of a response.

"In any case, you never should have taken the call. I heard you say, 'Mr. Updike is the superintendent to watch,' very unprofessional phrasing. In the future, you should forward all public relations calls to me and stick to your accounting."

Ms. Cole swept away leaving Tamara to fume. "I'd like to see how she'd turn that dead body into a good public relations statement. She'd probably claim Lincoln Township is starting a medical school in the kindergarten, and Mr. Updike has personally secured the cadaver."

The superintendent appeared in the hallway and strolled straight to Tamara's desk. "Excellent job on the report. Thank you for your hard work." Tamara smiled as her boss returned to his office.

A week passed with no new information. Tamara reported back to the club that speculation regarding Winston's absence had become the main conversation among coworkers since he hadn't shown up or called. Updike continued to behave in a perfectly normal manner, which roused Romy's suspicions.

The following Thursday, Tamara was sitting at her

desk when Detective Crooke opened the front door. Ms. Cole appeared out of nowhere. "Right this way, Detective. Superintendent Updike is waiting."

At least the woman sounds a little less haughty when greeting a police detective, Tamara thought. Instinctively, she ducked her head and reached for the phone to call one of the club members to let them know what was happening. Then she stopped. Better wait for more information.

Twenty-five minutes crawled by before the door to the superintendent's office reopened. Ms. Cole, Detective Crooke, and Superintendent Updike resembled a funeral dirge with their reluctant, uniform movements. "Excuse me, may I have your attention everyone?" the superintendent intoned.

He looks sad, but not nervous, Tamara thought.

"I am afraid Detective Crooke has brought us some very sad news." He paused. "There's no easy way to say this. I am sorry to tell you. Winston Dopplar has passed away."

The staff's respectful attention exploded in disbelief. "How did he die?" "Was it a car accident?" "He didn't look sick." Cindy began to weep. Mr. Updike gallantly handed her his monogrammed handkerchief and patted her on the shoulder. Ms. Cole promptly set a box of disposable tissues on the young woman's desk.

"He was found . . ." the superintendent paused and glanced at the detective, unsure of how much information he should share. Receiving a nod, he continued, "He was discovered on the jogging trail at Fort Harrison State Park," he paused again, "stabbed to death. Another jogger found him this morning."

"Winston?" Sylvia verified, sounding more surprised at who was dead than the news that a coworker had been murdered.

"No!" Cindy cried out. "He never knew the depth of my love for him," the girl confessed, sobbing.

This is more than I want to know, Tamara thought to herself, annoyed at the girl's histrionics over what must be an imagined affair.

"Are they sure it was him?" Roger asked.

"Yes. His sister identified the body. Detective Crooke needs to ask each of you some questions. Please give him your full cooperation."

Eyes shifted to Detective Crooke, dutifully in the background, carefully observing the various reactions: shock, disbelief, horror, as coworkers tried to absorb the news. Raw emotion showed on all faces except for one. On that face there was nothing. No surprise, no horror. Just closed off undercurrent—a resolve to show no reaction. Fifteen years on the force had taught him that this person would be a good place to start asking questions.

"Why don't I start with you?" the detective suggested with a smile. He paused and glanced at the brass nameplate her children had given her for Christmas. "Ms. Montgomery?"

"Yes, Tamara Montgomery."

"Superintendent, may we use your office for privacy?"

"Yes, of course."

Once inside Superintendent Updike's spacious office, Detective Crooke gestured toward a small round conference table. He waited until they were both settled, then looked directly into Tamara's eyes. "You look familiar?" Where might I know you from?"

Tamara smiled nervously, hoping he would not remember her having tea in Updike's living room. She never actually spoke to him that night and he was standing in the hallway more than twelve feet away. "Does forty-six in a thirty-five sound familiar?" she quipped.

"Did I stop you for speeding? I haven't worked traffic for more than twelve years," Detective Crooke commented. "I hope you are going slower now."

"I definitely am," Tamara promised.

"Good. Now tell me what you know about Winston Dopplar."

"Nothing really," Tamara stuttered.

"Really? Nothing?" Detective Crooke countered. "Didn't you work with him?"

"Well, yes, of course, I worked with him. We were both accountants. He was the senior accountant."

"So he was, in fact, your supervisor?" The gentleness of his tone almost belied the hidden accusation.

"That's true. He was . . . very good at his job, very thorough, put in lots of hours, often working late, especially during the last few weeks. He worked hard to get everything exactly right."

"And did he?" the detective questioned.

"Did he . . . ?"

"Get everything right?"

"He was an excellent accountant," Tamara stated firmly.

"Aha. Was he excellent personally?"

"I didn't know him personally," Tamara stated, daring the detective to contradict her.

He did. "Oh, come now, Ms. Montgomery, people have a personality even at work. What was Winston like?"

"He was . . ." Tamara floundered. She hadn't really liked Winston. He was a leech and a bore, and being dead didn't erase the possibility of his having been a thief.

"People hate to speak ill of the dead," Detective Crooke spoke in soft, soothing tones. "But the truth is all of us have our negative sides. Even then, we deserve for our murderer to not go free. The more we know about Winston, the better chance we have of catching the person who killed him."

Murderer. If she could be sure that the detective would find the real murderer, she would tell everything right this moment. Still, the cardinal rule of the club insisted once the ladies were involved, an iron curtain slammed shut on all outsiders. No exceptions. "I didn't know him well. He sometimes wanted to have personal conversations, but I . . . I tried to keep all conversations on business."

"Ah," Detective Crooked nodded. "I see. That must have been uncomfortable for you."

"A bit." Tamara wished the conversation was over.

"Do you know anyone else here at the office that may have been uncomfortable with him?

Tamara looked away, refusing to answer.

"All the women," he answered for her.

"But none enough to kill him!" she asserted.

"Someone did," he corrected.

Tamara flushed. "Are we finished?"

"For now. Thank you. You've been very helpful." Tamara left the office feeling a bit alarmed that she may have been helpful.

She had barely arrived back at her desk when the phone rang. It was Greg. As always, her estranged husband had impeccable timing. "Something's come up. I won't be able to pick the children up at school."

"It's two-forty now. You arranged to pick them up at three o'clock."

"Call the school and have them ride the bus home," he demanded.

"It's too late for that. The office doesn't deliver messages after two-thirty. The children have to be picked up."

"Can't do it. Something's come up," he repeated.

Tamara hung up wondering which one of his toy "somethings" it was tonight. "Roger, I need to go pick up my kids."

"Go ahead," he said. "There's nothing that can't wait to be finished until tomorrow."

"Thanks," she flashed an appreciative smile as she grabbed her keys. It occurred to her that, now that Winston was dead, Roger might be her new boss. She hoped so. Roger was great.

During the drive to the school, Tamara used her cell phone to once again call the ladies of the club. As the children pulled on their seatbelts she asked, "How would you like to meet some of your friends over at Chuck E. Cheese's?"

"Alright! Do you think the Rizkallah twins can come?"

"As a matter of fact, they can."

"Cool! I'll show the guys my new Pacers cards," Keith yelled.

Twenty minutes later the kids were playing air hockey and shooting baskets as the ladies of the club convened their meeting at a snack table.

"You are true friends. Thanks for agreeing to meet me at Chuck E. Cheese's. Greg is such a bonehead. Somewhere he missed the idea that parenting means meeting their needs, not fitting them into your schedule when it's convenient."

The friends murmured their sympathy. "Is it not getting any better?" Celina asked.

"Actually, it's getting worse," Tamara admitted. "Lately he's been threatening to petition the judge for custody."

"No judge would give him custody," Grace protested. "The man had an affair!"

"A whole string of affairs actually, but that doesn't matter. They don't consider morals when determining custody. As long as he doesn't break the law, immorality is not a problem. In fact, if it comes to a custody battle, his salary gives him the advantage. Plus, he has that five bedroom house, while the kids and I are living in a Cracker Jack box."

"I still don't understand how the court can give that huge house to him instead of to you and the kids," Grace shook her head; her strong sense of justice struggling to reconcile the facts with what she knew to be fair.

"I left him."

"Only because he refused to leave the house."

"But it gave him possession. Truth is, I wouldn't be able to afford that mortgage payment on my salary anyway. Now he's claiming that because of the divorce, he won't be able to afford the house. The judge said he can stay there as long as it's listed for sale."

"Good!" Romy pronounced. "Let him sell the house. You'll take fifty percent of the profit and buy a new place with no memories of him."

Tamara shook her head. "He has the house priced so far above the market, it will never sell."

"Why is he doing this if he doesn't really want the kids?" Grace rarely raised her voice. "Any real man would want his kids to live in a nice house."

"That's the saddest part of all. It doesn't have anything to do with the kids. He's doing this to get back at me. Greg wants everyone to believe he has the perfect life. When I left him, I shattered the image he had created of a perfect marriage. His company wants all of their top executives to have calm lives at home that do not interfere with their careers. My filing for divorce embarrassed him in front of the bosses. Greg hates to look bad more than anything. He's out for revenge."

"He can't be that petty!" Grace protested.

"He once ruined a coworker's credibility, and consequently, his future with the company, because the man pointed out an error Greg made in front of the boss."

Lara wiped a spill of salt off the table. "Do you have a good lawyer?"

"The best I can afford. I've only been in a courtroom once. That was for jury duty, and I didn't even get picked. If we go to court, I could lose the kids."

"Do you really think he'll do that?"

"I don't know. The other day when I reminded him it's not appropriate to take a five, seven, eight, and eleven-year old to see a PG-13 movie he said, 'You're not the perfect mother everyone thinks you are. I'm watching you. The first little mess up and those kids will be back with me where they belong.' That's why I'm so afraid of this whole thing with Winston and all that stolen money. I feel like I'm giving him ammunition when I breathe wrong." She sighed. "We can't do anything about Greg right now. Thank you for being such supportive friends. You guys are the best. Now, we better talk about Winston before the kids come back to the table. They found Winston's body on a running trail at the fort."

Chapter Five

"Do the police have any idea how he got there?" Romy asked.

"If they do, they're not telling," Tamara responded. "The police didn't even say whether or not they thought he had been killed there."

"Surely they can tell he's been moved," Celina started playing with the salt shaker.

Lara agreed. "His body would have stiffened into that crunched up position in the closet, but the rigamortis would have left by now."

"Sh! Not so loud! You never know who might be here," Tamara cautioned. She glanced around at the mobs of screaming children stuffing pizza into their mouths before racing off to ride miniature helicopters and motorcycles. Chuck E. Cheese's had, at least, two dozen rides, each with its own amplified sound, not to mention the noise from the games where balls crashed and horns announced winners. Up on stage, life-sized mechanical puppets blared out songs from the teen years of parents whose senses were too jarred from the noise to care. She realized caution was probably unnecessary.

"So what are we going to do?" Celina prompted. At work, she had a reputation for cutting off exhausting discussions and pushing committee members toward action.

"We still need to find out who stole money from the schools," Tamara reminded them.

"Maybe it was Winston, and now that he's dead it will stop," Grace suggested.

"Or maybe not," Tamara countered.

"I do have some information based on the infamous disc," Romy said. "Tamara was right. There's something funny about those records. The numbers have made strange jumps and dips over the past few months. At first I thought someone was totally incompetent."

"That would be me," Tamara made a face. "Those are the accounts I work on."

Romy nodded and went on. "But then I noticed a pattern. The rises occur in order, according to grade. For example, last October, Central Elementary's first-grade salary costs were high. In November, second-grade payroll at Riley Elementary went up. In December, third grade at Germantown Elementary and so on. The school always changes. Can't predict the school yet, although I may be missing the pattern. There's no logical explanation for this type of consistency except that someone is stealing." The other women nodded in agreement.

"Tamara, did you check the benefit records to see which employees have never filed an insurance claim or taken a sick day?" Celina asked.

"Out of the 5,032 staff members, 750 have never filed a claim, taken vacation days or called in sick."

"That's almost fifteen percent," Celina estimated.

"Fourteen point nine," Tamara specified.

"Too many," Celina tilted her head to one side as she thought about it. "According to our HR department at work, ten percent or less would be about normal. Actually this is good information because now we definitely know the money is being siphoned out through ghost employees. Knowing that should make catching the thief easier."

"Unless it was Winston, in which case the money is gone forever," Romy responded.

"At least it would be stopped," Lara glanced out at the play area to make sure her Johnny wasn't hanging upside down, endangering his head or other vital components of his anatomy.

"I did remember something when Detective Crooke was interviewing me today," Tamara responded.

"Detective Crooke? Not the same one who answered the Updike alarm?" Grace asked, startled.

"The very same," Tamara admitted.

"Did he recognize you?" Celina questioned.

"He thought I looked familiar, but wasn't sure from where. I told him he stopped me for speeding."

"Let's hope he bought that," Lara took a sip of her Diet Coke. "What is it you remembered about Winston?"

"During the two to three weeks before his death, he started putting in lots of overtime. He always put in late hours, but this was excessive, even for him."

"Perhaps he needed the extra pay." Romy commented.

"He was salaried."

"Maybe that's when he was stealing the money," Romy said.

"Or maybe he noticed the same things you did and figured out the thief's identity," Celina remarked. "Perhaps he confronted the thief or even tried to blackmail him and was killed for his efforts."

"It is possible. Do you think that's why Updike killed him? Blackmail?" Romy asked.

"We don't know Updike is the murderer," Tamara protested.

"The body was in his house. That's pretty good circumstantial evidence," Celina pointed out.

"I don't believe it," Grace disagreed. "He's too nice of a man. He couldn't have done it."

"So let's examine the possibilities," Celina theorized. One, Winston may have been the thief, and Mr. Updike may have killed him in a rage. Two, Mr. Updike may be the thief, and he killed Winston because Winston figured it out. Third, an unknown person may be the thief who killed Winston and planted the body at the Updike mansion."

"Why would the murderer plant the body at the Updikes?" Romy questioned.

"To implicate the superintendent."

Tamara shook her head. "Then who moved it out of the superintendent's house?"

"The superintendent did. He found the body, knew it would look like he committed the murder, so he moved it to the fort."

"You're reaching," Tamara dismissed the idea.

"Any possibilities you can suggest?" Celina countered.

"I'm thinking."

"Mom, Mom!" Elena's voice shrieked across the play area. Within seconds she had hurled her little body at her mother. "Quick! Fix my braid. It came out, and I have to get back. Caitlin from school is here. She's waiting. Faster, Mom."

Grace's manicured hands immediately began to form a French braid out of the flying strands. "Mom, Caitlin can throw a skeet ball straight into the center hole without missing. She promised to show me. Mom, Caitlin's in fourth grade, and she said she'd be my friend even though I'm only in third. Can you believe it? Thanks, Mom!" Grace's little dynamo bounced across Chuck E. Cheese's, disappearing through the crowd of bigger bodies.

"Grace, did you discover anything from talking to the teachers?" Lara resumed the conversation.

"Nothing atypical. Most teachers complain their salaries are too low."

"Romy, have you had time to check out the bank accounts of our suspects?"

"No, I focused on analyzing the disc, and haven't

had time to do anything else. Two of the appraisers I contract with called me to type additional reports. I'm glad to have the extra money, but the work load is also frustrating. The reason I started a word processing business out of my home was so I could be there for my kids. My daughter asked me to read to her yesterday, and I didn't have time."

"Sometimes I feel like all I do is run from one activity to the next," Celina agreed. "When you get too busy to read to your child, something is very wrong."

"I read to her at bedtime, but it would have been so nice to have just dropped everything and read to her right then," Romy added wistfully.

"There's just so much to be done," Celina lamented.

"But it doesn't all have to be done by you," Lara reminded her.

"No, but some of it does. That's the difficult part—separating the important from the crucial. Doing excellent work is commendable, but being available for those intimate moments with your children when their hearts are open and connecting to yours is vital. On our way home my boys will be overflowing with tales of everything they've done and thought of today."

Tamara spoke up. "Speaking of today's news, I forgot to tell you guys. When Superintendent Updike announced Winston was dead, Cindy, our data processing clerk, went into hysterics proclaiming that she was in love with him."

"Could she have killed him?" Romy asked the pertinent question.

"No. Why would she if she thought she was in love with him?"

"Jilted-lover syndrome?" Romy persisted.

Tamara shook her head. "I can't imagine anyone passionate enough about Winston to kill him."

"Some people are passionate about being passionate," Celina remarked.

"Do you think she was in love with him?" Grace questioned, tucking her burnished red hair back behind her ear.

"I think she has convinced herself that she was in love with him, but Cindy strikes me as the type of girl, woman really, because she is nineteen, who thrives on the emotions of lost love and missed opportunities. My guess is she always values whatever has been lost more than she treasures whatever blessings are in front of her."

"The question is, would she value it enough to create the loss herself," Celina clarified. "Some people do that."

"That's sick!" Grace protested.

"We are dealing with a murderer. I think it is safe to say the person is somewhat mentally unbalanced," Celina pointed out. "Or perhaps evil."

"Might Cindy be mentally unbalanced?" Grace directed her question to Tamara.

"Anybody could be mentally unbalanced, even us."

"Especially us," Celina quipped.

"How does the theft tie in if Cindy's the murderer?" Lara wondered out loud.

"It doesn't," Tamara asserted. "Cindy doesn't understand numbers well enough to pull off a theft with this kind of finesse."

"Then it's not a legitimate theory," Romy dismissed the idea.

"The theft and the murder may not be tied together," Lara cautioned. "We can't assume a connection. It's possible Winston was the thief."

Romy scowled. "I don't like puzzles where the solutions don't dovetail neatly. That's why I don't read mysteries. Too many authors write an ending that comes out of nowhere. In our case, if the thief is not the murderer, then where do we start looking?"

"We're obviously not going to solve this from a distance," Lara declared. "We need to be around the suspects to do a more effective job of detecting. Any ideas?"

"We can't hang out at the Administrative Office," Romy announced, stating the obvious.

Celina agreed. "Besides, Tamara's there. Her eyes are enough."

Lara used her straw to swish around the ice in her glass. "A more objective pair of eyes without any history with the suspects could give us a perspective we might otherwise miss. Romy is right. We can't hang around the administrative offices. We need some activity attended by the administration staff and several non-staff members so we don't look suspicious."

"I've got it," Grace announced. "The St. Patrick's Day Party at Mr. Updike's house on March 17th.

Tamara and the rest of the administration staff will be there in addition to parent and teacher representatives from each of the schools."

"I forgot about the party. I haven't even sent in my RSVP yet. I hate the thought of going back to the Updike mansion," Tamara shivered, "but I guess we must."

Lara nodded. "What excuse can we use to get the rest of us invited?"

"I should be able to come up with something," Grace promised. "I'll see Richard at a curriculum committee meeting tomorrow after school. Perhaps I can finagle invitations for each of you."

"No," Celina disagreed. "That would draw too much attention to us. We need to think of something else."

"What if you went as caterers or maids?" Grace proposed.

"I cook and clean enough for my own family," Romy protested.

"Still, that might be best," Celina considered. "We could stay in the background. Grace, can you get us hired for the superintendent's party?"

"I know his wife rather well," Grace admitted.

"If we're caterers, what will we do for the food?" Lara questioned.

"That should be simple enough," Celina reasoned. "We all have our specialties. The trick is for the five of us to throw a bunch of food together and make it look like a gourmet buffet instead of a potluck."

"We need to keep it simple or we'll never pull it off," Romy advised.

"That's what you always tell me," Celina sighed, "but I always seem to do things the complicated way."

"Yes, you do," Romy agreed. "Like the buffet you prepared for the Habitat for Humanity annual dinner. You must have had twenty different dishes."

"Twenty-two, but who's counting. I worked so hard on that meal. My friend Joanie and I were up until three in the morning the night before, mixing huge bowls of gourmet macaroni salad."

"I didn't know macaroni could be gourmet," Lara commented.

"This was. It had little chunks of apple and pineapple in a special sauce. Every dish we prepared for that dinner was gourmet. I was so proud. People praised the food right and left. Then, this one volunteer, who was a very big man, I mean this guy really knows his food, he said, 'Celina, this is great, absolutely wonderful.' My head swelled 'cause like I said, this man knows his food. Then he added, 'Where else can you get this much food for five bucks?' He sure brought me back down to earth." Her friends laughed.

"You may overdo, but any project you tackle is always done beautifully," Grace defended her.

"Thank you," Celina smiled.

"We can't make this dinner too simple," Grace continued. "Margaret Updike has a reputation for giving very extravagant parties."

"For drinks we can serve fresh ground gourmet coffees in two or three flavors," Celina suggested. "Irish cream, of course. Cinnamon's good, plus hazelnut or almond. Grasshoppers in the punch bowl would be appropriate for St. Patrick's Day."

"I thought beer was the Irish drink," Romy said. "Dye it green and serve it cold."

Tamara ignored the color suggestion. "Somebody better write all this down."

"I've got it," Lara flipped open a notebook from her purse and began scribbling.

Celina nibbled on a french fry. "Guinness is authentic Irish beer."

"Alright," Lara agreed jotting it down. "Grace, what about those colored chips you served at book club last fall? Were they purple or black?"

"Blue. They're not Irish, but let's serve bowls of those anyway. They're very in."

"I'm learning all kinds of things today," Lara commented. "I didn't know macaroni salad could be gourmet or that certain foods can be 'in.' I thought you either liked a food or you didn't."

"What else comes to mind when you think of Irish food?" Grace asked, drawing a blank.

"Irish stew," Romy announced. Her suggestion was met with silence. "The Irish are not known for their food," she defended her suggestion. "They are known for great parties."

"Don't they have a lot of sheep in Ireland?" Celina asked. "I'm sure I could find a recipe for mutton."

"Okay," Lara wrote it down.

"We need to serve some type of fish too," Celina added. "Salmon or mackerel. We can order those on the

Internet and have them flown in fresh from gourmet shops."

"Who is going to pay for all this?" Romy demanded.

"The Updikes, of course."

"Okay, ladies, we need something for dessert," Lara kept everyone on track.

"How about a choice of Irish cream cheesecake or Porter Cake?" Celina asked.

"Good," Lara added them to the list without waiting for discussion. "Plus colcannon and other assorted side dishes. We don't have to decide on everything tonight."

"Do you think you can find recipes for all of these?" Tamara worried.

"Celina's the cookbook queen," Romy responded. "She has more cookbooks than most people have food in the house."

"Okay," Lara summarized. "Romy, you start to work on individual financial summaries of the suspects. Grace, get us named as the caterers of choice. Celina, you organize the food, and I'll take care of renting the tables, dishes, etc. Anything we've forgotten?"

"What about decorations?" Celina asked.

"Do you think these people will pay us to decorate their house for a party?" Romy was flabbergasted.

"They will not only pay us, but they will pay us generously," Grace advised. "These are the kind of people who pay someone to decorate their family Christmas tree."

"Romy, let your imagination fly," Lara directed. "You and Tamara use your creative talents to come up with something to knock guests' socks off." She paused. "Well, ladies, looks like we're in the catering business. Anything else we need to talk about?"

"Who's going to check out the jogging trail site where they found Winston's body?" Celina asked.

"I can," Lara answered. "Any volunteers to go with me?"

"Me," Romy responded. "If you're off work tomorrow, why don't I pick you up at one o'clock? That'll give me enough time to clean house before we go."

"Sounds good," Lara agreed.

Celina stood up. "Five o'clock, ladies. Time for us to take our children home and solve the inexplicable mysteries of being a wife and mother."

Lara flashed her annual pass and accepted a map of the park trails from the guard before driving through the gates of Harrison State Park.

"Fort Harrison is beautiful any time of the year," Romy commented.

"It has a lot of history," Lara responded. "It was a prisoner of war camp during World War II. Most recently it served as a military finance center before being demobilized."

"How are we going to find the location where they found his body?"

"I'm not sure we can, but we need to try," Lara asserted, as she parked her car in a lot positioned at the start of a popular path.

Romy zipped up her warm ski jacket and pulled on

fur-lined gloves as she started up the snowy, wooded path. "Where will this trail lead us?"

"To the identity of the murderer, I hope," Lara quipped. "You look on the right side. I'll look on the left."

An hour later they ended back at the lot where they started. "Well, that led us in circles, literally as well as figuratively," Lara remarked. "What next?"

"I see a trail across the street," Romy observed. "Why don't we try that one?"

The two women followed the paved path through the barren trees, their eyes searching mounds of snow on either side of the trail for anything that could indicate a body had lain there. After a few minutes, the trail emptied out onto an open field. To the right, undisturbed snow covered the ground up to where the forest began again. A park road with only occasional traffic meandered along their left side. Up ahead, they could see a wooden fishing dock reaching out into the ice-covered lake. A solitary fisherman, content in his quest, sat on the frozen bank, the line of his pole submerged in a small hole he had chiseled with his knife. Without word or smile he nodded, indicating awareness of their presence, but not necessarily approval. Respectful of the fisherman's sacred quest, the ladies responded with a silent wave, curtailing all conversation until they were safely out of earshot. "Do you think we should have asked him if he noticed anything unusual lately?" Lara whispered.

"I'm not interrupting his fishing," Romy refused.

"You've got a point," Lara agreed. "Why don't we

try that path that leads away from the lake? The murderer might have felt safer in a more secluded area."

They continued walking for another half hour, finding only a couple of empty cans and a child's lost mitten. "Some mother is going to be looking all over the place for that mitten," Lara observed. "We'd better start back or we won't be home when the kids get off the bus. This time of day we're likely to get stuck behind some school bus, and the drive will take us forever." Lara pulled the crumpled park map out of her pocket and studied it for a minute. "According to this, we can take that trail over there to where it intersects with the trail we were on earlier and end up back by the car."

The two resumed their walk, moving at a faster pace now that they were thinking about beating the school bus home. Their eyes still roamed from side to side, but they had reached the point of having looked at the same basic view for so long that the only thing they really observed was the presence of more trees and more snow. They had almost reached the intersection where they would change paths when a splash of yellow color caught Lara's eyes. "What's that?" she asked moving towards it.

"Probably another lost mitten," Romy responded.

"It looks more like paper." Lara bent to scoop up a yellow strip of plastic with the letters RIME SCEN on it. "What does that mean?"

"Rime scen!" Romy interpreted. "Crime scene! This is a portion of that tape police use to block off an area where a crime has occurred so the evidence won't be compromised. We must be close to where they found Winston's body." She glanced at her watch. "We have exactly six minutes to find the spot and look for clues. Then we have to leave or our kids will come home to locked houses."

The search took less than sixty seconds. Set back about twelve feet from the path, the ladies found a slightly longer yellow strip tied to a skinny birch tree. "Police Crime Scene," Lara read. "You were right, Romy. This must be the spot."

"Unless it's from another crime," Romy suggested.

"Nothing else has been in the paper. What are the chances there have been two murders at the fort? This must be the spot. See how the snow has been trampled?"

"The snow looks like it's muddied more from police boots tramping over the area than it does from any clues the killer might have been kind enough to leave us," Romy commented. "That's odd. What kind of track is that?"

Lara bent down to get a better look. "It looks like a tire track, perhaps from a bicycle. A lot of people ride their bicycles through the park."

"Not through this much brush. They would at least stay on a dirt trail if they didn't want to ride on pavement. It must be how the murderer brought the body here."

Lara narrowed her eyes as she tried to picture the possibility. "The murderer couldn't have taken Winston's dead body from the mansion to the jogging trail on a bike. Even if no one noticed he was lugging a dead man, his bony body would be too wieldy to stay on the seat."

"You're right. That track is too thick for a mountain bike anyway." Romy paused to examine the area. "Here's another one! It's a pair of tracks running parallel about twenty-two inches apart. That's too close for bikes to ride together in this kind of brush. It has to be from something else."

"Do you think the police left those tracks?" Lara asked.

Romy shook her head. "I don't know how the police would have made those marks either. Winston would have been put in a body bag and carried out. They wouldn't have bothered with a stretcher out here." She glanced down at her watch. "We're out of time," she exclaimed. "The school bus will be on my street in less than twenty minutes. Come on."

Chapter Six

"Hello, Margaret? This is Grace Pappas. I'm calling to RSVP for the St. Patrick's Day party."

"You are coming, I hope?" The superintendent's wife spoke in low, rich tones.

"I'm looking forward to it," Grace continued. "Your parties are so much fun. You put an enormous amount of work into making them perfect."

"No trouble at all," the superintendent's wife lied.

"You always have every detail exactly right," Grace praised.

"You're so kind."

"Were you able to reserve the same caterer as last year?"

"As a matter of fact I was."

"Their food was incredible. What was their name?" Grace hoped her probing wasn't too obvious.

"Golden Palate."

"That's right, Golden Palate. You must have scheduled them a long time ago."

"Why, yes. Six months ago actually."

"See! Now, that doesn't surprise me at all," Grace continued. "I always mean to book a caterer like the Golden Palate, but I tend to wait until the last minute. My caterer provides excellent food, but doesn't have the reputation or client list of Golden Palate. They are, however, able to accommodate my last minute planning." Mission accomplished, Grace rushed to end the conversation. "I had better let you go. Just wanted to say how much I am looking forward to the evening."

"Thank you, dear. We are too."

Grace clicked the receiver and immediately dialed the Kelly house. "Romy, the caterer is Golden Palate. You're on."

"I love to be on," Romy confessed. She hung up and dialed the Updike number.

"Mrs. Updike?" Romy asked in a frazzled voice. "This is Myrna Kleinman, with Golden Palate. I am so sorry to bother you, but I'm afraid we have dreadful news."

"Tell me about it," Margaret encouraged.

"Must have been all this freezing weather we're having. A water main in our kitchen here at Golden Palate burst."

"A water main?"

"Yes. Totally flooded our kitchen and shorted out the electricity. All the freezers are on the blink. The insurance company says it will take months to sort out. We won't be able to cater anything for weeks."

"We must get it fixed," Margaret responded as if she were announcing the solution. "The superintendent and I are giving a St. Patrick's Day party on the seventeenth. How soon can the repairmen be there?"

"They can't. You must have heard about this on the news. People across central and northern Indiana have lost heat and water. The repairmen are giving priority to apartments and individual residences. It's quite a disaster."

"I had heard that some homes had lost heat, but not anything about it being a disaster situation. This sort of thing does happen throughout the Midwest every winter. It doesn't seem to be any worse this year than normally."

"It may not be an official disaster, but it has temporarily put us out of business. The damage cannot be repaired in time for us to cater your party."

"We can't possibly change the date of the party. Perhaps you could rent refrigerator units," Margaret suggested.

"There's just no way to do it." Romy's voice still sounded frazzled but a note of firmness had crept in. "You must find another caterer."

"I don't believe there is enough time to do that." Margaret's tone shifted to flattery. "Not to mention no other caterer would have your talent or reputation. There must be something we can do."

"It's all we can do to stop the water damage from spreading," the voice insisted. "Again, I am sorry for the inconvenience."

"Yes, of course," Margaret conceded. "So sorry for your misfortune. Can you suggest another caterer?"

"I really can't. The companies I know are already booked for St. Patrick's weekend. You might ask your friends if they know of a catering company that's not busy."

Grace didn't have to wait long for the phone to ring. She listened as Margaret explained her predicament. "Of course, I have the caterer's number right here."

"Wonderful!" Margaret hesitated a moment before proceeding. "We don't need to mention this slight glitch to the superintendent. He has so much responsibility at work that I do my best to keep our home life running smoothly."

"Of course," Grace agreed smiling that their plan was working so well.

Romy rubbed her kitchen cabinets with Murphy's Oil Soap while she waited for Margaret to call. She was near the refrigerator when the phone rang. "Bon Appetit catering," she answered in a German accent that sounded unnervingly like her immigrant mother.

"Yes. We can do Irish party for you March 17th. We had cancellation. I have menu ready for party."

Margaret Updike's smooth voice attempted to take control of the conversation. "Actually, I have a menu

I've spent quite a few hours preparing." She laughed apologetically. "I was thinking of potato soup, corn beef and cabbage—very authentic recipes."

"I give you lamb, salmon, Irish Whiskey cake, wonderful feast—everything Irish."

There was a pause at the other end of the line as Mrs. Updike realized she had no choice and conceded that her carefully planned menu would not be on the table at this year's party.

"About the decorations . . ."

"Your house will be Irish beautiful." Romy cut in. "We take care of everything."

"Okay," Margaret Updike's worry evident in her reluctant response. Clearly the woman was anxious at the thought of a German caterer planning her Irish celebration.

Romy took pity. Both of them knew Mrs. Updike did not have the option of another caterer at this late date. "Not to worry," she comforted Bon Appetit Catering's only client. "Everything will be perfect."

Romy dialed the Golden Palate. "This is Mrs. Richard Updike," she announced. "I am afraid we need to cancel our St. Patrick's Day party for March 17th.— No, the superintendent's fine, just a scheduling problem. Thank you for asking." Romy frowned. "Yes, I understand we forfeit the $500 deposit. Again, I apologize for any inconvenience." She hung up muttering to herself. "The Updikes will expect their deposit refunded. Lara better remember to work that in when calculating the catering cost."

Tamara had the children fed, bathed, and in bed. Greg had agreed to watch the children, and she wanted to give him as little to complain about as possible. "Thank you for staying with the kids so I can go to my book club."

"No problem," Greg responded. "Oh, by the way, change of plans. Can't do Disney World during their spring break. That's when I'm going to the national convention."

Tamara glanced at the family calendar hanging on the wall beside the telephone. She had printed the words *National Convention* across the second week in June months before she had discovered the existence of Paige, Tiffany, and untold others. "The national convention isn't until June," she corrected.

"Oh, you're right," Greg paused to recover his verbal fumble. "Doesn't matter. It still isn't convenient for me to go during spring break. We'll have to change the date."

"Are you thinking of right after they get out of school or later in the summer?"

"I'm not going to Florida in summer. Too hot! We'll go the third week in May."

"But they're still in school then."

"So they'll miss a week. They can make it up," Greg dismissed her concern.

Tamara chose her words carefully, determined to keep the conversation on a civil note. "That's pretty hard on them. Lincoln Township doesn't excuse an absence for family vacation. Even if their individual teachers allow them to make up the work, their grades won't be as good because they'll be doing double the work."

"You always like to make everything difficult. I'm taking the kids to Disney World during the third week in May and there's nothing you can do about it."

"If you don't want to go in summer, then why can't you take them during spring break? That's a slow time for your office anyway."

"I have other plans that week."

"What plans?" Tamara bristled.

"Not that it's any of your business, but a friend and I are flying to St. Thomas. She already has her vacation time scheduled. I tried to be a nice guy and spare your feelings, but you insisted, so now you know."

"You claim to be so strapped for cash that you can't help with Debbie's braces. How can you afford a vacation to St. Thomas?"

"You are not going to control how I spend my time or my money, Tamara! Here's another example of your crazy behavior that broke up our marriage. If you weren't so controlling, I wouldn't have to support two households. I pay so much child support, you ought to pay for Debbie's braces and our trip to Disney World. What do you do with all that money I give you anyway?"

Tamara's resolve broke. "You don't pay *me* anything. You help support your children, and you are behind on that."

"I'm not going to argue with you. Are you going to go to your silly book club or shall I leave now?" Greg had an uncanny ability to agitate the worst in her and then reply with a calm and reasonable voice as if totally amazed at her ravings.

If the club had been a social evening, Tamara would have skipped for the sheer pleasure of telling him to get out of her house. Instead, she squelched her anger and kissed the children good night.

Tamara felt worn out from her confrontation with Greg and deeply in need of the solace that comes from an evening with friends. She walked into the hallway of Celina's brick, cottage-style home and chucked off her boots, leaving them to drop on the gray slate tile. "It's freezing out there. Indiana winters last too long!" she complained.

"That's funny coming from a native of Minnesota," Romy retorted from her cozy position on the English chintz sofa. "You grew up with higher snows and lower wind chill factors.

"I'm amazed everyone up there doesn't just hibernate the winter away," Celina added.

"We come out for the Mall of America," Tamara confessed, crossing the room to warm her hands beside the roaring fireplace. She took a deep breath, soaking up the genial atmosphere. White iron chandeliers, Queen Anne furniture upholstered in romantic Laura Ashley fabrics, soft yellow throws, and half a dozen pillows of assorted sizes gave the room a dreamy feel, at odds with the outside climate and Tamara's internal turmoil. "Any woman is willing to come out in a blizzard for over five hundred and twenty stores."

"Not I," Lara disagreed.

"Me neither," Celina handed Tamara a cup of peach-flavored tea. "If I don't have it when the snow starts, you can't convince me I need it. Maybe it's the reality of the everyday office grind, but I love when a good snowstorm forces me to burrow in with my family. What was that term yuppies popularized a few years ago? Nesting? Yuppies no longer nest, but I still do."

Tamara accepted the tea and sank into a Cambridge armchair. For the moment, nothing mattered but the delight of wallowing in friendship.

"I would happily brave a snowstorm for a good mall," Grace tore a twig of grapes off the fruit platter.

"Grace, is that a new dress?" Celina admired her friend.

"Yes, I picked it up at Von Maur last week. Do you think it's too short?"

"Not for you."

"Grace is one of the few women in her thirties who still looks good in a mini-skirt," Tamara approved.

"I'm only twenty-nine," Grace corrected.

"The baby of our group," Lara replied.

"Adult women do not look good in a skirt eleven inches above the knee," Romy said.

"I don't wear dresses that short!" Grace objected, looking down.

"No, but some people do. Haven't you seen women who wear clothes intended for teenagers?" Tamara asked. "Why on earth do they leave their houses looking like that?"

"Because," Celina answered, "they think they look good."

"Well, they don't, and someone ought to tell them."

Lara's brown eyes danced. "Imagine walking up to a stranger and saying, 'That dress does not look good. For the sake of everyone, please, go home and change.'"

"That's what they need to hear," Romy approved.

"Same thing is true with hairstyles," Celina added. "Sometimes I get the urge to say, 'Honey, there is a fine line between chic and stupid, and you have crossed that line'."

"Go home!" Lara repeated.

Romy continued, "Fashion license is one thing. Bad taste is another. Average people should not walk around in clothes intended for supermodels."

"Grace could pass for a model if she were about three inches taller," Celina observed. "She still looks like a girl."

Grace chuckled. "Evidently not enough to fool the more discriminating viewer. I was chatting with my neighbor down the street who has a first grader. The mother was interested in hearing about the art crafts I do with my students, so I mentioned that we finger painted in kindergarten today. Her son, Sean, glared as if he had caught me in the biggest fib and said, 'You are too big to be in kindergarten!' " The ladies laughed.

"En guard!" Two high pitched voices challenged the peace of their conversation. Plastic swords flying, Celina's eight-year-old twins fought their way into the living room three steps ahead of their father.

"We've come to say goodnight," Samar Rizkallah assured them. His clipped English accent revealed years of attending British schools while growing up in East Jerusalem. Celina's husband had the curly black hair and handsome Mediterranean features of his Palestinian ancestry. He wore a slightly modified version of the Arab moustache. The genetic influence of a Scottish great-grandmother had bestowed somewhat light skin.

"We had a men's night out," the miniature duelist announced with pride.

Andrew nodded. "First, Dad took us to McDonald's. Then he taught us to sword fight. Peter, Dad, and I are the Three Musketeers."

"Wanna see us duel?" Peter offered.

"Absolutely," Grace, the kindergarten teacher enthused.

Shouts of "En guard!" and "Take that!" filled the air amidst much swashbuckling and clashing of swords. Just as one of the young cavaliers was about to take a hefty blow to the head, his mother grabbed him up to safety.

"I was going to cut his ear off the way Saint Peter cut off the soldier's ear in the Bible," little Peter objected.

"Not until you can put it back on the way Jesus did,"

his mother instructed firmly. "It's time to sheath your swords and say goodnight." Reluctantly, the twins obeyed.

An oven timer dinged. "Dinner is ready." Celina invited.

Walls the gentlest tint of rose added more warmth than color to the eat-in kitchen. Z-bricking above the counter mimicked the floor's Italian ceramic. The glow of a 19th-century chandelier flicked shafts of light off brass pots hanging from an overhead rack. Heavy, black iron skillets invited guests to believe in home-cooked meals.

After asking God's blessing on the food, Lara described the crime scene she and Romy had found at the park. "Any idea what could have made those tracks?"

"Could they have been wheelchair tracks?" Celina suggested.

"A standard adult wheelchair is about a foot and a half wide," Lara responded. "We have some at the hospital that are extra wide. The marks Romy and I saw on the trail couldn't have been more than twenty-two inches apart."

"Is it possible they were made by one of those adult-size tricycles?" Grace asked. "My neighbor Mrs. Bernacchi rides hers up and down our street whenever the weather allows it. Wonderful exercise for her."

"Possibly," Romy said, her voice filled with doubt.

"We may have to find our answers elsewhere," Lara concluded. "Tamara, tell us about the people who work in the accounting office."

Tamara helped herself to the poppy seed salad before passing it on. "As you know, Winston Dopplar is . . . was the senior accountant. Superintendent Updike claims Winston was an accounting genius, but he seemed more annoying than brilliant." She hesitated for a moment before continuing. "I feel so bad talking about him now that he's dead. The truth is no one in the office liked him, except perhaps Cindy. She craved the attention he gave her. What else could she have admired? He used to say and do the stupidest things. I don't know if he didn't have any social sense, common sense, or if he just didn't care what people thought."

"What could he have done that was so repulsive?" Celina pumped her.

"For one thing, Winston always had to top everyone. If you had a cold, he had pneumonia. If you saw a Pacer at the grocery store, he saw the whole basketball team at the mall. I once heard him insisting he had eaten more at a buffet than Roger, our third accountant, did. Childish stuff that nobody cared about."

"That is annoying, but if he was good at his job, people still should have respected him," Lara reasoned.

"It was more than being overly competitive. His whole manner implied he thought himself smarter than everyone else. He would explain the same accounting principle over and over and over again until I thought I was going to scream. I don't know how someone so socially ignorant could wear such a smug look."

Grace's eyes widened in surprise. "Tamara, that is so unlike you."

"I feel horrible about it, especially now that he's dead. He was so strange. Last fall, Winston came in to work with a six-foot stick. He said he sprained his ankle playing basketball, but he wasn't using it to walk. He just wanted the attention. He even carried it into the lunchroom, turning it sideways to maneuver into an empty chair. He whacked poor Roger on the back of the head."

"I would have paid to see that," Celina admitted, laughing.

"You're making this guy up," Lara protested.

"Not even a little bit. You had to wear old clothes if you went to lunch with him."

"Why?" Lara's voice was guarded.

"Because sitting next to him at a meal almost guaranteed you would get slimed. Last Christmas, Mr. Updike took all the staff downtown to The Skyline Club on top of the AOL building for lunch. Very elegant place. Award-winning chefs, beautiful views of the city, live piano music. Everyone dressed up except Winston. He forgot to wear a tie, so the maitre'd supplied him with one. Most of us had already filled our plates from the buffet and taken our places at the table when he returned with a dish piled high with shrimp and cocktail sauce. The man is so bony he hit the table with his knees, shaking the table and splashing cocktail sauce onto Mr. Updike's shirt."

"I hope it wasn't white," Romy winced.

"White cotton broadcloth, monogrammed, and starched to perfection."

"What did Richard say?" Grace asked.

"He didn't say anything. He just dabbed his Ralph Lauren shirt with a cloth napkin and tried to get it out. Winston was totally oblivious. He finally settled into his chair, then looked over and noticed Mr. Updike rubbing the stain and said, 'Oh, you splattered yourself, didn't you?'"

The ladies dissolved into laughter.

"It doesn't sound as if Winston was bright enough to pull off this kind of embezzlement." Lara observed. "He sounds dumb."

"But if Superintendent Updike thought he was a mathematical genius . . ." Romy's protest trailed off.

Lara finished the sentence for her. "Perhaps his coworkers were not giving him enough credit."

"Maybe we didn't," Tamara admitted.

In the silence that followed Celina suggested they move into the living room for dessert.

Romy and Lara settled comfortably onto the English chintz sofa facing the fireplace. Grace pulled a rocker closer to the Indiana brick hearth as Lara pulled out her notebook and pen. "Tamara, besides Winston and Mr. Updike, who are the other people in your office?"

"About twenty people work in our building. Sylvia is the receptionist. She's been with the township administration for four years now. Sylvia is somewhere in her early fifties, pleasant and efficient. Cindy is a payroll clerk, only nineteen and very immature. She's been with us for almost nine months."

"How long ago did you start noticing changes in the logs?" Celina asked, as she served Midnight Mint Bars and poured steaming tea from the Laura Ashley teapot her friends had given her for her thirtieth birthday.

"Eight months ago. Mr. Updike also has an administrative assistant, Amy Cole—excellent at her job. Ms. Cole is from the old school of total dedication to her employer. She's even a bit snobbish about the fact that her boss is a man who is independently wealthy and doesn't have to work for a living. She likes to imply he's doing it for 'the good of the people,' not because he needs the money."

"He doesn't need the money, that's true," Grace agreed. "His family has money. His wife has even more. She's from 'old money' out east, where the age of currency really means something."

"I don't care how old my money is as long as it spends the same," Romy confessed.

"Does Updike's assistant, Ms. Cole, need money?" Lara questioned, jotting down her notes.

"She makes a good salary, probably saves quite a bit."

"My kind of woman," Romy approved.

"She doesn't have anything to spend it on," Tamara asserted.

"You don't know that," Celina countered.

"Work is her life. She's not involved in anything else."

"Anything romantic going on between Ms. Cole and Mr. Updike?" Romy asked. "Inquiring minds want to know."

"There are always those kinds of rumors any time a woman is loyal to her male boss. They grew up together in a small northern Indiana town."

"Good grief," Grace interrupted. "Have you ever seen his wife? She's gorgeous—never a hair out of place."

"Mrs. Updike comes in the office about once a week." Tamara turned back to Romy. "To answer your question, I haven't seen anything inappropriate."

"It could be Ms. Cole likes the prestige that comes with being the top dog's administrative assistant," Romy commented. "Some people get their power vicariously. We had a secretary like that when I worked at Bray Realty. She was a snob about office protocol, especially, everything going through her to get to the branch manager."

"There are snobs everywhere," Celina observed. "Just the other day my husband called to make lunch reservations. Evidently information gave him the number for the university chancellor's office instead of the restaurant called Chancellor's. When he asked for lunch reservations, a very haughty secretary informed him. "Mr. Charles Morgan is chancellor of the entire university. He does not do lunch.' "

"What a snob." Romy laughed.

"No sense of humor, which is even worse," Celina scrunched her face in distaste.

"Tamara, how would you describe Ms. Cole?" Lara refocused on the theft.

"Annoying, but harmless."

"She's not harmless if she's in love with a married man," Lara disapproved.

"No, but at least we can be sure they aren't having an affair," Grace asserted. "Richard is definitely in love with his wife. The Updikes are very close."

"What does the superintendent think of Ms. Cole?" Romy asked.

"He recognizes her as a competent assistant who could be making double the money working for a major corporation. He's very grateful for her loyalty."

"If she could be making twice as much working somewhere else, there's definitely something going on somewhere," Romy insisted.

"No way," Grace argued.

"Grace, it's not human nature to keep working for a company where there is no chance of advancement and probably little raise except the yearly cost of living adjustment."

Celina piped up, "Actually, that describes at least eighty percent of the American workforce."

"Is there anyone else in the office that would have access to changing names or numbers in the computer?" Lara questioned.

"Only Roger. He has worked for Lincoln Township for over six years. I like working with him. I'd even go so far as to say he's a friend, although we don't socialize outside the office. We've worked on several projects together. He's organized and always pulls his share of the work. I had hoped he would get the promotion a year ago when the position of senior accountant became available. Unfortunately, they hired Winston from outside the township."

"Anyone else with an opportunity to be in the room where this information is kept?" Lara followed up.

"Principals, teachers, volunteers, and auxiliary staff float in and out of the building all the time."

"It could be an outside job. Who is the custodian?" Romy prompted.

"We use a cleaning service. Their staff changes from week to week."

"All right then, this is what we need to do." Lara's voice was crisp as she sketched out a plan, clearly expecting success from her fellow club members. It was easy to imagine Lara's swift, meticulous actions during a code blue. "We need more information. Grace, listen to gossip in the teacher's lounge. Find out if anyone is overly concerned about money. Romy, get those bank records and see what you can find out about these people. Make it a detailed report. We need to know who is spending extra cash lately."

Romy reached for a chocolate mint on the end table. "I can get all this information you're asking for by tapping a few computers, but I won't have time to do it for several days, and then you'll have more information than you can decipher in a month."

"We'll divide that up. It will be interesting to see if the theft stops now that Winston is gone," Lara turned to Celina. "How are plans for the party coming?"

"All the food is ordered from gourmet shops around

the Internet world. I charged it on my Visa, so let's hope the Updikes pay before the end of this billing cycle."

Romy spoke up. "I told her payment is due in full the night of the party. I already opened a DBA account under the name Bon Appetit Catering."

"Let's hope they don't check us out with the bank."

"Grace, have *you* ever checked your caterer out with the bank?" Romy questioned.

"Now that you mention it, I never have."

"Tamara, how are the decorations coming?"

"Fine. Romy designed them. She and Celina are going shopping for the materials on Saturday. Romy and I start sewing on Monday."

"Great!" Lara approved. "We should be ready to roll on the 17th."

Chapter Seven

Tamara added and subtracted numbers until the marching band fund-raiser receipts balanced. She appreciated the mundane tasks that forced a normalcy about her actions. The last nine days had provided a fever of excitement that she neither needed nor desired.

Work supplied a brand of relief. Even busy days at the office had limits to them. Tamara performed specific duties, and then she went home. Only occasionally did she need to stay after hours or put in overtime on the weekend. On the other hand, the simple logistics of single parenting crowded her hours like a merry-go-round that wouldn't stop. Routine tasks, all with a sense of urgency, clawed at her, demanding attention and taking her away from those four beautiful children she loved most. She often felt pressing trivialities replaced the substantial and busyness crowded out the significant.

That had been the biggest benefit of being married to Greg. A successful salesman, he earned a good salary, allowing her to stay home with the children. Two months before her first child was born, Tamara resigned her position with a downtown Indianapolis accounting firm. She never considered going back to work while she had small children. That is, until she found out about Greg's "indiscretions" as polite company referred to adultery. *Indiscretion*—that word sounded more like a reference to forgetting Ms. Manners' rules of etiquette than a description of destroying one's family.

Revelation of his first affair devastated her. She analyzed her every behavior since the day they were married, trying to discover how she had failed as a wife. News of the second fling prompted her to update her resume and think about how she and the kids could make it without him. Knowing the turmoil a divorce would put her children through kept her in the house despite not believing Greg's promise it would never happen again. Discovery of a third woman found her prepared and well established in her new job. Tamara and the kids were out of the house before Greg was home for dinner.

Tamara sighed, missing the freedom to greet her kids at the door when the bus dropped them off or to surprise them with an after-school trip to the park or McDonald's. *Tonight we will have a kickback evening,* she promised herself as the phone rang. We'll pop corn, play board games, and maybe even rent a movie.

The phone rang. It was her lawyer. "This is Marilyn Caruso. I wanted to alert you to a new development.

Greg's lawyer notified me they are filing a motion to change custody."

Tamara felt her insides gel. Fear she had fought to suppress surfaced. Unsure how to quell the panic, she said nothing as the lawyer continued.

"This only means that for whatever purpose—whether to intimidate you or to use as leverage in the division of assets, he has made the official request. It has nothing to do with the judge's decision. Don't let this scare you."

"What do we do?" Her question came out as a whisper.

"We ignore it. From everything you've told me, custody of four children would greatly inconvenience this man who does not like to be inconvenienced. He's looking for a reaction. If we give it to him, we play right into his hands. First, we need to see what he's after. Think of this as fighting a crocodile. You never fight a crocodile on his own turf. Instead, coax him out of the water where you can see how big a tail he's thrashing around. That's what we're going to do with Greg. Don't argue with him. Don't try to convince him of anything. We need to see the size of this crocodile."

Tamara hung up the phone and pushed back from her desk. Where was that normalcy she had been feeling a moment ago? In an attempt to force it back, Tamara snatched up her completed report and darted up the back stairway to the second floor where she tapped on Ms. Cole's door.

"She's not there," Sylvia called out as she passed. "I

saw her in with Mr. Updike. If that's the federal grant report, she was tapping her foot for it an hour ago."

"But it's not late!" Tamara protested. "It's due tomorrow."

Sylvia grinned. "I think she saw you working on it this morning and couldn't stand the thought of a report coming in before she requested it." She laughed as Tamara crossed her eyes. "Better leave it in her in-basket to save yourself some grief." Sylvia strolled on down the hall toward the copier.

Tamara glanced at the in-basket hanging outside the office door. Ms. Cole was rather persnickety about reports not being left where anyone could walk by and see them. "I don't know why she cares," Tamara grumbled. "We are a government institution. Our reports are supposed to be public record. All the same, annual reviews are coming up. I don't want to give her any ammunition to lower my merit raise."

She advanced into the administrative assistant's office. The office looked as if it had been designed to meet specifications in a book entitled *The Efficient Office.* Desk, chair, and computer were positioned ergonomically correct. Four-drawer file cabinets fit squarely against the wall doing their part to maximize efficiency. A mini-shredder sat on top, with a wastebasket located below to collect the discarded strips of paper. How like Ms. Cole, who seemed to derive a sense of importance from classifying the trivial as top secret. The only sign of a personality revealed itself in a snapshot of the superintendent shaking hands with Ms. Cole at a staff recognition dinner.

It amazed Tamara to see how anyone could be so organized in such a limited area. Personally, she always blamed her own lack of organization on the need for more space.

She reached out to place her completed work on the desk when a legal size document caught her eye. It was a report similar to the one she had saved on the X-Box 360 Codes disc.

Stunned, Tamara picked up the spreadsheet to gain a closer look. Streaks of yellow highlighted the precise pattern Romy had discovered. Where did this come from? Did someone else provide Ms. Cole with this proof or did Ms. Cole herself know what Tamara had done? Had the superintendent seen the disc and made a copy?

Tamara flung the papers back down on the desk just as an unyielding voice demanded, "May I help you?" Before her stood the administrative assistant, looking as righteous as a Crusader poised to pounce on a pagan.

"No! I brought you the federal grant report. I knew you'd be looking for it today."

"And did you think *this* was the federal grant report?" Ms. Cole snatched the spreadsheet off the desk as her eyes bore through Tamara.

"No, I . . . no, I didn't."

"Then you won't need *this,* will you?" A grim smile crossed Amy Cole's face. Her eyes never left Tamara's as she fed the highlighted report into the shredder.

"No," Tamara agreed, confused, but believing conformity to be the safest course. "I won't need that." Quietly, she backed out of the office, pulling the door behind her as if that action would provide additional protection from the menace on the other side. Once in the hall, she leaned her head back against the wall and tried to make sense out of what had happened. Why did Amy Cole have her own spreadsheet highlighting the discrepancies? More importantly, what prompted her to shred it? Not fear. Her eyes had gleamed with vindictiveness as she destroyed the paper, almost as if she were taunting Tamara. What point was the woman trying to make? Did Ms. Cole think Tamara was the one stealing the money? Was that her way of saying she could prove it any time and didn't need that piece of paper to do so? Or was Amy Cole the thief? Did that make her Winston's murderer? Was she flaunting the crime and daring Tamara to prove it? Could the shredding have been a threat or a warning for Tamara to keep her mouth shut?

Tamara took a deep breath as a chill shuddered through her body. Glancing down, she realized she still held the federal grant information in her hand. Disgusted, she slipped it into the in-box located on the wall outside Ms. Cole's office.

"Wait!" a voice whimpered.

Tamara turned to see Cindy, the data processing clerk quickstepping toward her. "I have to talk to you."

"Now?"

"Yes. It's about Winston."

"Not now," Tamara protested, exasperated. She didn't think she could tolerate listening to Cindy's tale of unrequited romance one more time.

"I have to talk to someone about it. You're the best friend I have here."

"You don't talk to your girlfriends about Winston?"

"I don't have that many friends." Realizing how pathetic that sounded, Cindy rephrased her narrative. "I mean, yes, all the time, but none of them ever knew him. They didn't know the man that he was." Her voice caught a tragic tone.

Caught between feelings of impatience with the melodrama and pity for anyone who lacked friends, Tamara tried a delaying tactic. "Why don't you and I go out to lunch next week? We can spend the whole hour talking about your feelings for him?"

Cindy's face lit up. "That would be wonderful!" Then the clouds came back. "If I last that long. How can I live without him?"

Tamara shifted her eyes downward to avoid revealing her impatience. Regardless of how silly she thought Cindy's behavior, the girl was entitled to her own emotions without being ridiculed. "I'm sure you'll be fine. You have to face the fact it takes a while to recover from the type of loss you've had."

"I'll never get over losing Winston. We were soul mates. No one here knows it," she whispered, "but Winston and I were dating. We kept it secret because of his position as the head of accounting. Winston said if people knew we were so intimate, they might think he was giving me preferential treatment. He said they might even fire me. I was willing to give it all up for him, but he said he wouldn't allow me to make that kind of sacrifice. Wasn't he wonderful?"

Tamara focused on the girl driven by an obvious desire to be seen as the grieving lover. She remained silent, trying to think of a more compassionate response than, "That scum! You're better off without him!"

Cindy interpreted the silence as understanding and continued, "We were so close. He used to tell me all his thoughts and feelings. No one knew him like I did. That shows how much he trusted me, don't you think? He must have loved me. A man would never trust a woman with his deepest thoughts if he didn't love her, would he?"

The victim of lost love had her full attention now. "Cindy, are you saying Winston confided in you?"

"Intimately. We confided in each other. I trusted him with my every idea."

"Did he trust you with his?"

"Of course." Cindy didn't like the implication their love affair was anything less than total oneness of heart. "He told me all about his difficult childhood, how he struggled through school. Not academic struggles. He was brilliant. But the other kids teased him. I told him they were jealous. They didn't have his gift. He could practically smell numbers. He knew if they were right or wrong."

"Did he talk about the numbers here at work?"

"Yeah. He always wanted everything to line up exactly. Winston hated inconsistencies. He always insisted every account had to balance to the penny."

"Yes, he did," Tamara encouraged further confidences. "He was an extremely conscientious senior accountant. Did he mention if the accounts were balancing to the penny?"

"He talked about that a lot. Sometimes they did. Sometimes they didn't. The whole thing was confusing. I don't understand accounting. One day he would say everything looked fine. Other times he would be very upset and claim nothing made sense. The morning before he died, he told me he was sure someone had to be stealing."

Tamara glanced over her shoulder at Ms. Cole's office door, wondering if the administrative assistant was listening from the other side. She had not heard one sound from the office since her exit. Taking Cindy's arm she propelled the girl closer to the busy accounting floor. "Did Winston say whom he suspected?" she whispered.

Cindy hesitated. "At first he thought it might be you. You do have access to all the books and accounts," she defended her lost love.

"Perfectly understandable rationale," Tamara soothed.

"I'm also sure that's why he flirted with you. I saw him flirt with you. At first it hurt my feelings, but then I realized he must be trying to get information and find out if you were guilty." Cindy's glare challenged her to dispute the statement.

"Of course."

"Sort of undercover work."

"Hmm." Tamara brushed that thought aside as definitely not worth thinking about. "How did he know it wasn't me?"

"You kept drawing attention to the problem. You wouldn't have done that if you had been guilty."

"True—very astute of him."

"Winston had strong people skills. He could always read people. That's a talent I don't have."

Tamara looked with compassion at the nineteen-year old so desperately in need of affirmation. "I'm glad Winston could talk to you, Cindy. You were good for him."

The girl nodded tearfully. "We would have been real good together."

Tamara paused as Sylvia brushed past them on her way up the front stairs. "What did he think after he realized I wasn't the thief? Did he have any other ideas who might have stolen the money?"

"Winston had ideas on all kinds of things," Cindy avoided the question. She lifted her chin, smug with the knowledge that she and she alone, knew the thoughts and mind of that magnificent man, Winston Dopplar. Typically, she enjoyed telling not only whatever information came into her possession, but pretty much every thought. For months she had wanted to shout it from the rooftops that she had a boyfriend. Only Winston's threat of breaking off the relationship had compelled her to keep their dating a secret. Now that the moment had come to share what she knew, she vacillated. She hesitated giving up her prize, knowing that once she did, her singular hour of glory would dim. Cindy relished this rare moment of power. "I don't know that I should discuss his ideas with you."

"Winston wouldn't want the thief to go free," Tamara coaxed.

Cindy lifted a stubborn jaw and remained silent.

"If you tell me everything he told you perhaps you and I can figure it out together. He wanted the thief caught. He would want you to carry out his final wishes. Perhaps that's something I can help you do."

Cindy shot her a sly look. Tamara had always been kind to her although a little impatient at times when Cindy didn't understand instructions quite as fast as Tamara seemed to think necessary. That was one of the things Cindy had liked so much about Winston. He never tired of explaining the same idea over and over to her until she understood. Her heart wrenched. Never would she find another man so patient. It still amazed her that he had paid so much attention to her. Cindy knew she wasn't the brightest girl around, but that never seemed to bother Winston. He was brilliant enough for both of them. Listening to him, Cindy felt kind of smart too. Should she trust Tamara? The data processing clerk had originally approached Tamara because she knew from Winston that Tamara was innocent of the theft. Still, Winston had flirted with the woman. Although it had been to gain information, the truth was the flirting had bothered Cindy. While his words remained solely hers, a portion of Winston's thoughts belonged to her alone. If she gave them up, she would be giving up a part of their intimacy, their only intimacy, although no one else needed to know that. Should she forget about Tamara and tell the police directly? Winston hadn't wanted to do that. He wanted to solve the mystery himself. If only Winston hadn't been stabbed by some nutcase on the jogging trail. If he were here, he would know exactly what to do.

"Did he tell you who the thief was?" Tamara persisted.

"No," Cindy admitted. "But he said money always leaves a trail. He said it several times."

Tamara refrained from mentioning a movie that also came to mind as a source for that quote. Calling on the patience she used with her children, Tamara rephrased the question. "Did he mention possible suspects or explain how he was going to follow the money trail?"

The door to Ms. Cole's office swung open and the administrative assistant strolled out with papers for the superintendent to sign before he left for lunch. "Get back to work, girls. We don't have time to stand around here and gossip." She sailed passed them.

Cindy automatically started to move in the direction of her desk. Tamara reached out, gently pulling back on the girl's arm. "Cindy, please . . . anything at all?"

"He said the bank accounts prove who stole the money. I have to get back to work. Did you see how angry Ms. Cole looked?"

A defeated Tamara returned to her desk. She felt like shaking the girl by her shoulders until she disclosed everything Winston had ever murmured to her. Cindy had a stubborn streak, though. The more anyone pushed her, the more obstinate she became. Tamara had noticed that personality trait when trying to teach Cindy how to process accounting reports. Temporarily leaving her alone would probably be the most effective action. Cindy loved to tell everything she knew. Depriving her of an audience today might bring her in search of one tomorrow.

"Tamara, do you mind putting a copy of the semester end report on my desk?" Mr. Updike's smooth voice interrupted her plans.

"Certainly, Mr. Updike. I have a copy here. Would you like it now?"

"No, just put it on my desk. I'll take a look at it as soon as I get back. My wife is taking me to lunch at The Garrison." He grinned as a stunning woman with champagne-blond hair walked over to join the conversation.

"I have to steal the man away every so often or I'd never get a minute alone with him," Margaret added. "I received your RSVP for the St. Patrick's Day party, Tamara. We're looking forward to having you as our guest."

"Thank you. I'm looking forward to the evening. How are plans coming?" Tamara asked, all the while thinking Mrs. Updike should be asking her that question.

"Wonderful. Everything is proceeding according to schedule."

"It wouldn't dare do otherwise with my wife in charge," Richard Updike quipped. "The woman's a born manager. She keeps my world as near perfect as possible. Can't imagine what I would do without her."

"You wouldn't be having a St. Patrick's Day party, that's for sure," his wife teased back. "He looks at the big picture," she informed Tamara. "I take care of the details."

"Sounds like you make a good team," Tamara commented wistfully.

"We do all right," her husband grinned.

"Tamara," a stage whisper commanded everyone's attention. Cindy leaned forward as if unaware others could hear her words. In reality, she had decided it was time others recognized her rightful place as the woman in Winston's life. "Winston was the love of my life. I'll never have another confidant like him. Thank you for taking the time to comfort me," she added, hoping it would encourage others to do the same.

Instead of the sympathy she imagined, everyone standing there felt embarrassed for her. Several colleagues winced. Ms. Cole actually snorted. Roger looked down to hide the expression on his face.

"Oh dear," Sylvia murmured, and then as a deterrent to further public confidences, she offered, "I bought a box of chocolate pecan turtles from the South Bend Chocolate Factory. Would you like some, Cindy?"

"I can't! I'm deathly allergic to nuts!" Sobbing, Cindy fled to the restroom leaving her coworkers in doubt as to whether the tears were a result of Winston's death or her allergy to nuts.

Tamara rushed to explain. "Cindy enjoys talking about Winston. They were . . . close."

"She's taken his death rather hard," the superintendent observed.

"Yes," Tamara agreed. "Yes, she has."

"Mr. Updike, I have everything in place for the June 22nd conference Lincoln Township is hosting." The administrative assistant decided enough time had been spent discussing the silly girl and redirected the topic of conversation. "You'll be pleased to know I have arranged for Howard Gardner to give the keynote address on multiple intelligences."

"Thank you. I appreciate all the hard work you put into this meeting. You always go way beyond the call of duty. I have no idea how you snagged Howard Gardner as a speaker."

"You certainly are a treasure, Amy," Margaret Updike added. "I personally am grateful for the way you keep him in line at work. It's all I can do to keep the home and social life in line with his desires."

The assistant acknowledged the wife with a nod Tamara was unable to read. If there was any tension between the two women, Mr. Updike was oblivious to it. With his hand in the small of his wife's back, he guided her out the door.

Tamara rejected the theory of Mr. Updike and Ms. Cole having an affair. Ms. Cole might run around the office as if she ruled the world, but the moment Margaret Updike strolled through that door, the assistant became insignificant. "His wife is more than a beauty on his arm," Tamara thought. "She has a style and presence all her own. Ms. Cole may be useful for business, but she's only an office appendage."

On Saturday, Romy stood inside the foyer of Jo-Ann's Fabrics and Craft Superstore waiting for a tall woman with honey-blond hair to enter. She waved a gloved hand. "Celina, over here. Ready to spend your Saturday morning shopping? Pat is taking the kids for haircuts, so I am free to shop 'til I drop. Or until one-thirty, whichever comes first."

Celina hugged her. "Samar took the twins to the YMCA. All three of them about fell over when I suggested they go play basketball. I usually have a long list of jobs for them to do on Saturday mornings. They wondered why I didn't today, but were afraid to ask questions in case I changed my mind."

Romy brushed snowflakes off her three-quarter length herringbone wool coat. "Two and a half hours should give us enough time to buy the decorating supplies we need for the Updike's St. Patrick's Day party. I also want to tell you what I learned going over our suspect's bank records."

"Let's hear it!" Celina demanded as she steered a shopping cart toward the fabric section.

"I completed a review of Superintendent Updike's personal bank records shortly after midnight last night. I almost called you right then. His account has a strange pattern of cash withdrawals and deposits. Two Fridays a month, a large sum of money, always in the thousands and always ending in the number seventy-seven is withdrawn from the bank. Within three or four days, almost the exact amount is re-deposited."

"The amount of the withdrawal always ends in seventy-seven?" Celina frowned.

"Sometimes he withdraws fourteen thousand and seventy-seven cents. Sometimes he withdraws twenty-one thousand and seventy-seven cents. Once he withdrew seven thousand seven hundred seventy-seven dollars and seventy-seven cents. Regardless of how many thousands he takes out, the amount always ends with seventy-seven cents."

"That is strange. What did you mean, almost the exact amount is re-deposited?" Celina questioned.

"The amount deposited three or four days later never ends with seventy-seven cents. It always rounds up and ends in zero." Romy took a shopping list out of her purse. "Why would you continually take money out of your account just to put it back in a few days later?"

"Orderly withdrawals sound like some sort of payment or blackmail," Celina mused. "Or he could be spending that money and replacing it with township money."

"Tamara had quite a conversation with Cindy yesterday." Romy filled Celina in on the processing clerk's dramatics. "Cindy quoted Winston as saying, 'Follow the money.' "

Celina scrunched up her nose. "That sounds like a bad B movie."

Romy selected a spool of gold thread. "Winston sounds like a bad B movie all by himself."

"What is Mr. Updike spending the money on? Someone needs to follow him from the bank on Friday and find out where he's going." Celina suggested.

"That someone will be either you or Lara. Updike would recognize Grace and Tamara. I need to spend every spare minute sewing these decorations. We may only be replacement caterers, but I can tell from the places they write checks that Grace is right. The Updikes expect high quality."

Celina fingered a green cotton print. "It's amazing what you learn about a person by hacking into a few computers."

A shopper turned to stare, and Romy laughed as if at a joke. Then she grabbed Celina's elbow to steer her behind tall bolts of wedding lace.

"Keep your voice down before someone turns us both in to the police."

Chapter Eight

"Sorry. You amaze me. I can't believe the stuff you find out."

"I get the job done." Romy admitted, lifting her chin.

"You do indeed," Celina agreed. "Where do you think he's getting the money?"

"No idea. The checks going out of his account reflect regular household payments—gas, water, electricity, fifty-five hundred a month for a mortgage payment, plus they make large monthly donations to various charities."

"Fifty-five hundred a month for a mortgage payment?" Celina gasped.

"I know. Doesn't it make you sick? Their electric bill is seventeen hundred a month."

"Somehow I can't bring myself to feel sorry for them," Celina commented wryly. "He's not making that

122

kind of money as superintendent. Where does he claim his money comes from?"

"Inheritance. Grace checked with an expert on Hoosier genealogy. According to Jean Perney, Updike's family settled in Indiana as fur traders over two hundred years ago. The family still owns a large farming corporation in the northeast part of the state, mostly corn and soybeans. His great-uncle and cousins run the farm, although the superintendent does receive yearly dividends. This is in addition to the lump sums dispersed at the death of his parents and grandparents."

"From the way Grace and Tamara have described them and the pictures I have seen in the society pages, I can't imagine the Updikes down on the farm," Celina mused.

"A picture of the Updikes experiencing the farm is closer to gentleman farming than the sharecropping your grandparents did. Grace told me Margaret Updike arranges for the family to celebrate Thanksgiving at the old farmhouse. Caterers cook a traditional feast for the extended family. When there's enough snow on the ground, they even take the horses out for a sleigh ride. She creates the perfect holiday for her family."

Celina sighed. "How does she do that? I love traditional celebrations. My goal is for our family holidays to resemble a Currier & Ives picture or a Thomas Kinkade painting. I always have this mental image of what I'm striving for, but the reality never completely matches my aspirations. I run out of time to make it happen. When I do have every detail correct, I end up exhausted for three days afterward."

"Why do you do it?" Romy asked curious as to why her friend would put herself under such pressure when it wasn't necessary.

"I do it for our family. I give so much of myself on the job, I want to give my family the best I can offer too. I want everything to be perfect for them."

"Life isn't perfect. Do something nice, but a little easier on yourself."

Celina laughed. "That's exactly what I tell myself every time I pull out the cookbooks. I say, 'Celina, make it a simple seven-course meal.'"

"Seven courses! Oh, honey! No wonder you're tired when company arrives! People love to be invited to your home, but you don't need to be exhausted. Your guests would enjoy the evening every bit as much if you made only the main course or the dessert gourmet and everything else simple and easy. Celina, there's a reason why no one compares to Martha Stewart."

"But I *want* to do everything as well as Martha Stewart."

"Then you need to hire her staff." Romy checked her list before pulling a bolt of Irish-green cotton off the shelf and sticking it in their cart. "There wasn't anything else unusual in the Updike family account; however, I did find something interesting on Ms. Cole."

"Spill it!" Celina demanded.

"Ms. Cole has quite a bit of money, over two hundred and fifty thousand in her savings account. A firm named Townsend and Rowan deposits an average of

$5,000 into her account every month. Supposedly she has stock in Wal-Mart."

"How long has she been receiving the deposits?"

"As far back as I could check. The IRS would have more information if I could access their files."

"You couldn't?"

"I tried, but with no success. I couldn't bypass their security," Romy whispered, obviously disappointed with herself.

"Where is Townsend and Rowan located?"

"New York City." Romy selected a bolt of black felt before pushing the cart over to the appliqué aisle. "Do you think Ms. Cole is blackmailing the superintendent?"

"Maybe. She could be the thief. Or she and the superintendent may be in this together."

"Could be. Well, we'd better get this shopping done. We won't have another opportunity to do it. Picture this," Romy enthused, "bouquets of fabric shamrocks on every table. We'll place life-sized leprechauns in humorous poses around the house, and suspend a glittering rainbow from the vaulted ceiling with a pot of gold waiting at its end."

"A pot of gold?" Celina repeated raising an eyebrow.

"Actually an old witch's cauldron left over from Halloween. But we'll spray paint it gold and fill it with chocolates."

"I'd prefer chocolate over a bunch of old money any day," Celina grinned as they headed for the checkout counter.

* * *

As Tamara stepped through the doors of Lincoln Township Administration on Monday morning, her mind automatically refocused on Cindy. She felt torn between wanting to know if the girl had remembered something critical and a desire to run from hearing an ode to Winston. She concluded that since listening to the latest rendition of *Love Lost* was probably inevitable, she might as well hope for some useful information. After a weekend of mentally replaying every word Winston had ever uttered, as Cindy undoubtedly had, the girl might have remembered something significant.

A quick glance at Cindy's desk revealed the young woman had not yet made her morning appearance. 7:55 A.M. She should be in pretty soon. The girl might be scatterbrained when it came to performing her duties, but she always arrived on time to sincerely try.

The smell of Maxwell House and leather boots dripping with snow slush permeated the air. Members of the office staff who were naturally morning people zipped from desk to desk, requesting information, emphasizing deadlines and generally annoying staff members who were not morning people. Ms. Cole, queen bee to the early workers, flew through the common areas, ignoring those for whom she had no immediate task. Tamara engulfed herself in solitary work, effectively blocking out the sounds of banging file drawers, reams of copy paper being ripped out of their packaging, and competitive brags and complaints pertaining to her coworkers' weekends.

Cold swept in as the front office door opened.

Tamara looked up expecting to see Cindy. Instead, she locked eyes with Detective Crooke. "Oh, great," she muttered. *When Cindy does get here, we won't have any place to talk without him around. Maybe I can take her to lunch. That would give us almost an hour of uninterrupted time.*

His eyes never leaving hers, Detective Michael Crooke sauntered up to Tamara's desk. "May I have a word with you, Ms. Montgomery?" His authoritative tone indicated it was not a request. Ms. Cole appeared and hovered nearby.

"Yes, of course," Tamara stammered. "How may I help you?"

"Somewhere private would be better," he commanded.

"This way, Detective," Ms. Cole obliged. "The superintendent is in a conference. You're welcome to use my office."

Tamara's eyes moved to the face of the administrative assistant. A look of gleeful triumph adorned the woman's face. *She turned me in,* Tamara surmised. *She's not the thief after all; she thinks I am. No. Look at that face! I've never seen such evil on a face, such maliciousness. She knows Updike is the thief, and she's framing me. She's so proud of herself she could do a little jig down the hallway.*

Nose slightly upward, posture like a trained pointer, Amy Cole sallied forth with delight. "Is there anything else I can do for you, Detective?" Amy asked as she escorted them into her office.

"No, thank you. You've been very helpful."

Brief disappointment crossed the older woman's face. Then, with a slight nod, she backed out of the office, pulling the door to as she exited.

Silence filled the room like a suffocating gas. *Don't say a word,* Tamara instructed herself. *Find out what he knows first. Maybe he's going to accuse you of the theft, but not the murder. Listen to everything. Admit nothing.*

Michael Crooke motioned for Tamara to have a seat before easing himself into a chair. "I called Superintendent Updike this morning and explained I'd like to know more about Winston's daily schedule and habits. He suggested you would be a good person to speak with since you and the senior accountant worked so closely together." Detective Crooke paused. When Tamara didn't say anything, he continued, "Did you notice any changes in Winston's habits during the weeks prior to his death?"

"Nothing other than the extra evening hours I mentioned before. Has something new come up?" Tamara probed, half afraid questions might indicate some sort of guilty admission.

"Nothing new, but now that the autopsy report has been completed, we're ready to move forward with the investigation."

Tamara nodded.

She felt as if the policeman was baiting her as he added, "Of course, we know he didn't die on the jogging trail."

"Do you know where he was killed?" she ventured.

"I'm not at liberty to go into that," he brushed her question aside. "You don't seem surprised he didn't die on the jogging trail, Ms. Montgomery."

"Winston wasn't the type to jog. He was . . . too . . . clumsy."

"Ah. Then, of course, there's the issue of the ice pick. Why would a murderer have an ice pick with him . . . or her . . . on the jogging trail? And if he took it with him, why would an ice pick be the weapon of choice? Why not a butcher knife or at least a steak knife?"

"You hadn't mentioned he was stabbed with an ice pick," Tamara countered, feeling like she had side-stepped a trick question.

He ignored her defensive tone. "There's another reason I wanted to speak with you privately, Ms. Montgomery. I'm afraid I have some sad news. Cindy Patterson, your data processing clerk, died Friday night."

"NO!!" Tamara blurted out. "Not Cindy murdered too?" Tamara stopped herself. She felt lost in a jumble of unasked questions and blurry realities.

"I don't recall saying she was murdered," Detective Crooke demurred. "She died of an allergic reaction to nuts."

"She accidentally ate something with nuts in it?"

"Suicide. She wrote a note on her computer screen, which was still up and running."

"No." Tamara disagreed, shaking her head.

"No?" Detective Crooke probed. "Why not?"

"She wouldn't harm herself. Besides, with two deaths in the same office, why would you assume the second to be suicide?" Tamara tried to push him closer to the truth.

"We're exploring all possibilities. As of yet, the evidence is inconclusive. Why would you assume the two deaths are connected?" Detective Crooke baited her. "According to what Superintendent Updike told me over the phone, Cindy was emotionally distraught over Winston's death. Would you agree that was true?"

"Yes . . . but that would have made her less likely to commit suicide."

"Young women have been known to become dramatic and kill themselves over the loss of a young man."

"That's just it!" Tamara continued to protest. "Cindy was dramatic. She loved being dramatic. All of those histrionics made her more alive than I have seen her in the entire time she worked for Lincoln Township. She finally had an experience of her own requiring deep feelings. I don't know if they came before or after Winston's death, but I believe they were genuine."

Detective Crooke remained silent. As if cued, Tamara raced to fill the silence. She needed safe words that would force the police to investigate Cindy's death further. "Don't you see?" she continued in a soft voice. "Cindy relished tragedy, especially romantic tragedy. She was forever reading those kinds of books—in fact, I suspect it was the only type of book she read. This was her opportunity to live the drama. Why would she have given that up?"

"Perhaps she wanted to increase the dramatic effect with a fake suicide attempt and simply miscalculated the amount of nuts she could safely eat. The labeling revealed they contained almonds. The coroner confirmed she died of an allergic reaction to almonds. Perhaps she imagined nibbling on a couple cookies and then lying down for a long nap from which someone rushes in to wake her just in time. The stage was perfectly set. She even propped a long stem white rose against the computer screen to draw attention to her note. Might not her goal have been to have become a real-life sleeping beauty?"

"I don't think so." For the first time, Tamara began to doubt her own conclusions. Could it have been a stupid accident?

They sat in silence for a moment, then Detective Crooke leaned forward, "Why are you taking Cindy's death so much harder than Winston's?" he whispered.

"Because Winston was an idiot!" she burst out in frustration. "Cindy was so young, so very naïve. She trusted everyone to be exactly what he claimed."

"Are you exactly what you claim?" the detective asked.

Weariness wiped out the fear on Tamara's face. "I'm exhausted, Detective. I have lost a coworker who once told me I was the best friend she had in Lincoln Township. If you have no further questions, I would like to be released."

"Released, Ms. Montgomery? You were never brought in for questioning. I simply wanted to tell you about your clerk in private."

Not trusting her mind to think clearly, Tamara stood, bone-weary exhaustion evident as she moved toward the door. She paused at the threshold, closing her eyes to block the sight of Amy Cole standing in the very spot Cindy had stood just three days before.

Cindy's death intensified the club's drive to solve the mystery. Although the continuing theft exonerated Winston's memory, the second murder changed their objective from protecting the township funds to a strategy for rendering the murderer powerless. Although terrible, the theft itself had not appeared life threatening. Winston's death was clearly unplanned, a crime of the moment possibly provoked by his own arrogance and stupidity. But now Cindy was dead. All five of the ladies agreed it was not suicide, but murder, intent on self-preservation. Club members knew the hour had come to take an aggressive approach. They congregated in Romy's kitchen, strategizing their next move, while their children built a snow fort in her front yard.

"We haven't been able to discover who the thief is or who killed Winston. Let's consider who might have killed Cindy," Tamara suggested, as Romy placed a pot of steaming tea and a plate of cowboy cookies in the middle of the kitchen table.

"What's the difference?" Grace questioned, picking up a cookie.

"Nothing probably," Tamara admitted. "Possibly a different angle to mull over. Cindy died of an allergic reaction. There's no way she would have eaten those cookies voluntarily, but how can you force someone to eat cookies they don't want to eat?"

"I don't think you can without holding a gun to their head," Lara answered. "A cookie isn't something you can slip into a person's mouth and force them to digest. She must have had some reason for cooperating. Do you think she didn't realize the cookies had almonds in them?"

Tamara shook her head as she poured herself a cup of tea. "I can't imagine her not reading the ingredients on the package. Being allergic to nuts was part of her identity. At work pitch-ins, she questioned people about what was in their dish, always reminding them that she was allergic to nuts. 'All nuts,' she would say, 'not just peanuts, like some people.' "

"So everyone at the office knew about the allergy?"

"No one could have escaped knowing."

"So what do we do now?" Celina brooded.

Tamara crumpled her napkin. "We need to get into Cindy's apartment. Maybe we can find something the police missed."

"Get into Cindy's apartment!" Grace protested. "See! I knew this would happen! I knew the moment we broke into the first house that there would be others to follow. We have crossed the line. We are as bad as the people we are trying to catch."

"We may be bending the rules a little bit, Grace, but we're hardly as bad as a murderer or thief," Celina admonished.

"Breaking into someone's apartment is still against the law."

Romy spoke up. "Technically, I don't think you can call it breaking into someone's apartment. She's dead, so it's not really her apartment anymore."

"It's still breaking and entering!" Grace raised her voice in objection.

"Grace, you are such a rule follower!" Celina declared.

"Yes, I am. That's a good thing!"

"Within reason," Celina modified.

"So who's going into the apartment?" Romy queried.

"I guess it should be me," Tamara reasoned.

"I'd go with you," Romy apologized, "but I have to finish this data processing assignment. My client wants it in two days. You can borrow my tools. I'll show you how to open the lock." Romy pulled the steel gray box from her handbag.

"That would be great. Thank you."

"You keep burglary tools in your purse at all times?" Grace exclaimed in a horrified whisper.

"One never knows when they'll come in handy," Romy defended herself. "Just last week I helped a sweet old woman who had locked herself out of her car."

"A sweet old woman?" Grace repeated skeptically.

"She was probably even a widow."

"How kind of you, not to mention how talented. You can break into cars as well as houses. Your creative skills know no end."

"It's not really a separate ability," Romy grinned modestly. "The mechanical principles are the same."

Tamara poured another cup of tea and switched the subject. "Romy, this tea is delicious. What flavor is it?"

"Almond." The two women stared at each other.

"That's it," Tamara announced.

"She didn't eat the cookies at all," Romy declared. "They were a red herring! Now you know what to look for in Cindy's apartment."

"Evidence of almond tea," Tamara agreed. "Show me how to use those tools."

A simple entry lock guarded Cindy's apartment rendering Romy's detailed instructions unneeded. Tamara's blue and white Indianapolis-Marion County Public Library card did the trick. "I wonder if it would make Grace feel better to know I didn't use any special tools," she mused. Easing the door open, she ducked inside the apartment.

The blinds were tightly closed, effectively hindering her from seeing to move about the room. Tamara pulled out the pinpoint laser she had borrowed from her son and switched it on. A powerful half an inch beam of light revealed a single spot of the room clearly, but left everything else in total darkness. "That's a lot of help," she grumbled under her breath. Running back to the car for the standard-size flashlight she kept in her glove compartment would increase the odds she might be seen entering or leaving the apartment. She would have to make do with this silly little laser.

Tamara sidestepped the coffee table moving toward the faint outline of the living room picture window. She adjusted flimsy vertical blinds to let in slivers of light from the parking lot. That's better. Now I can see what I'm doing. Her eyes focused on the front door as she turned away from the window. For a moment she thought it was moving. My imagination must be playing tricks on me. Still unsure, Tamara took a step forward. With eyes straight ahead, she rammed into the coffee table she had avoided moments before. "Ow!" she cried out automatically. Bending down, she rubbed her calf. Another slight movement caught her eye, and she froze as the door opened yet another inch. Light from the hall revealed a thick, black stick-like object coming around the corner of the door. The shape of an oversized baton and the hand carrying it formed a black silhouette against the hall's brightness. Tamara felt the malady of terror creeping up her back, struggling to come out her throat. The next instant an intense beam of light exploded directly into her eyes, blocking out any hope of identifying her adversary.

Chapter Nine

"What are you doing?" a voice challenged her.

"Grace?" Tamara verified.

"Right here," a Southern voice drawled.

Tamara heaved a sigh of relief. "Get that thing out of my eyes." The light switched off. Tamara took another deep breath. "You know what I'm doing. Why are you here?"

"I was worried about you."

"Why?"

"I was afraid I distracted you from learning how to use Romy's tools, so I thought I'd better come help you."

"You wouldn't know how to use them either. By the way, how did you get in?"

"My credit card."

"Grace Pappas! You know how to break into a locked home!"

"My own, not anybody else's. Daddy showed me how years ago just in case I ever locked myself out." Feeling a shade uncomfortable, she added, "I'm only here for support. I still don't condone breaking and entering."

Tamara smiled into the darkness. "As long as you're here, does your support extend to helping me look for clues?"

"Only because it will get you out of here sooner." Grace reached into her pocket and pulled out two pairs of disposable first-aid gloves. "Here, put these on."

Tamara's eyebrows shot up. "You have latex gloves?"

"I bought three boxes to send to a missionary midwife in Madagascar who spoke to our church. She said they were washing and re-using their disposable gloves because they don't have enough. That's disgusting, but they have no choice. It's a good thing I forgot to take them on Sunday. Put them on." She stretched a pair over her own hands. "With these on we won't have to worry whether or not the police will be back for fingerprinting. I'll buy the missionaries a new box."

Grace switched her flashlight back on and motioned Tamara forward.

Cindy's living room furniture consisted of a 13-inch TV, a worn sofa, and two chairs, one which looked too uncomfortable to sit in, and the other which looked too comfortable to get out of. A selection of poster reprints including Kandinsky's *Painting with Green Center* and Heade's *Magnolias* leaned up against the wall, bought in a flurry of art appreciation but abandoned in favor of music appreciation before they could be hung. Three inches of an afghan-in-the-making drooped over barely used roller blades. A variety of props implied busy days, but an absence of snapshots with friends and family portraits underscored a lonely life.

Well-thumbed stacks of *Glamour* and *Seventeen* magazines stood in the center of the end table. An eclectic collection of CDs crammed the stereo cabinet in a haphazard way preventing the glass door from closing completely. Nothing was organized, but everything appeared to have been shoved out of sight. An empty plate with a few cookie crumbs rested on the latest copy of *People magazine*.

Sorrow tinged Tamara's voice and her eyes welled with unshed tears. "Her death seems more real here."

Compassion filled Grace's face. She slipped her slender arm around her friend's shoulders without saying anything.

"Why would someone . . . kill her," Tamara spat out the words. "She was nineteen, still a teenager. The girl didn't even have a life yet. She playacted whatever emotions she thought she should be experiencing."

"Perhaps it was the way she playacted emotions that led to her death," Grace's voice was gentle.

"What do you mean?"

"Perhaps the killer thought the emotions she was expressing were based on specific knowledge or information. She may have come across so intensely emotional that the killer thought she knew more than she did. Her murder may have been a mistake."

"A mistake!" The word even tasted bitter.

Grace continued probing. "What could Cindy have implied she knew?"

"She might have implied she knew anything, including the killer's identity."

"That's probably what got her killed."

Sick at heart, Tamara turned away. "Let's get this over with."

"It looks like she picked up in a hurry for company," Grace observed, as she pulled a white sock out from under the sofa cushion where it had been tucked.

"The guest may have been the murderer," Tamara commented, as they moved toward the eating area.

In lieu of a dining room, a Value City table and chairs marked the entrance to the galley kitchen. Gold-colored appliances matched the linoleum and counter top. The lazy Susan stood half open, revealing clear plastic containers of sugar, flour, and generic tea bags. Breakfast dishes dirtied the sink.

"Look at this," Grace commented, as she eyed two coffee mugs beside the sink, their handles at perfect perpendicular angles to the sink. The cloth they had been dried with was folded neatly beside them. "The coffee mugs are clean, but her breakfast dishes are still dirty. Why be fastidious about cleaning the mugs, but not the breakfast dishes? Why would she fold the cloth used to dry those mugs when she tossed all the other wash cloths and drying towels in a heap on the sink?"

Tamara shook her head. "She wouldn't. People rarely behave outside of their predictable habits. Those mugs must have had the almond tea in them. The murderer must have washed them. What I don't understand, though, is how the murderer provided the tea at Cindy's apartment."

"Hostess gift," Grace responded. "A decorative canister of tea makes a perfect gift when someone has invited you over for afternoon tea. The murderer probably substituted almond tea for whatever was inside."

"Cindy would have read the label, but she probably wouldn't have been able to tell almond tea from hibiscus. She wasn't much of a tea drinker," Tamara admitted. "Let's look for the canister."

"Nothing here," Grace announced, as she closed the last veneer-coated cabinet.

"Let's look through the rest of the apartment."

Three feet of undesignated space imitated a hallway. The door to the left revealed the bedroom, to the right stood a restroom. The bath was lined with containers of fruit-scented bubbles, herbal shampoo, and a conditioner that guaranteed the most advanced biotechnology, while reassuring it had never been tested on animals. A stiff air-dried washcloth and an uncapped tube of whitening paste perched on the sink. The room appeared disorganized enough to be natural. No clues in sight.

Grace stopped at the threshold of the bedroom. A pile of assorted size-nine shoes at the closet edge evidenced a hasty search. Drawers were half-open with panty hose hanging over the edges. "Did the murderer ransack the apartment?"

Tamara picked her way through clothes strewn across beige carpet. "I don't think so. Cindy must have dressed in a hurry and had trouble deciding what to wear. It couldn't have been for work on the weekend, and as far as I know, she didn't attend church. I wonder if she was trying to impress the murderer. Perhaps she knew he was coming." Tamara glanced around the bedroom. "This looks like my Julie's room. Just seeing it gives me the urge to pick up the clothes."

"Resist that urge," Grace commanded. "We need to get out of here before somebody finds us. I'll check her dresser drawers and closet. You look around the bed."

Tamara began sorting through a stack of papers spread across the nightstand. Two of the papers fluttered to the floor. "Gloves make it hard to put papers back in the same place," she complained. They completed the search without finding anything.

A few minutes later, Grace eased the apartment door shut behind them. "I need to swing by my parents' house to pick up Elena, but after that I'm going home. Would you like to come over for a cup of tea?"

"Thanks anyway. I think I need a quiet evening at home."

"I understand. Hey, where are your keys? You didn't leave them inside Cindy's apartment, did you?" Grace questioned.

"Right here," Tamara lifted them out of her coat pocket. "I left my purse at home, so I wouldn't have so much to carry."

"You know it's illegal to drive without your license, don't you?"

Tamara hugged her. "Thanks for coming with me, Grace. I'm glad you were here."

Grace grinned. "Hey, what else are friends for if not to commit grand larceny together?"

"Actually, it's only breaking and entering. Grand larceny involves theft. We didn't take anything."

"Hah! I knew it was breaking and entering." Grace retorted, as she headed for her car.

Ten minutes before noon the following Friday, Lara parked outside the Fall Creek branch of United Savings and Loan, waiting for a man Tamara described as tall and distinguished looking with the faintest thread of silver highlighting his brown hair. At his appearance, Lara followed the gentleman into the brown-brick building, lingering at the service desk while pretending to fill out a deposit form. The noise of paper rattling and customers shuffling prevented her from hearing the exact amount of his withdrawal, but confirmed what she most needed to know. Richard Updike was the one making withdrawals from his bank account. He drove straight back to the office without making any stops and without speaking to anyone.

At exactly 5:01 P.M., the superintendent exited Lincoln Township Administrative Offices. The moment the door swung shut behind him, Tamara punched in the cell phone number of a car located in the parking lot.

"Are you available to babysit?" she asked.

"In place and ready to go," Celina confirmed. She glanced at Lara, sitting beside her who nodded.

The two women watched Richard Updike stride through the clear winter day. Boyish grin on his face, he whistled as he clicked his key chain to unlock his car. Within minutes, his silver Mercedes-Benz glided from 56th Street onto I-465. The Sebring convertible followed discreetly behind. The quest was on.

Celina steered into the right lane, careful to keep an anonymous distance. Rush hour traffic clogged the expressway, making it easy to remain invisible. Celina drummed her thumbs against the steering wheel. "I was hoping it wasn't him," she confessed. "I hoped that perhaps someone else was fooling around with his bank account, making deposits and withdrawals."

"Why would anyone do that?"

"I don't know, maybe an attempt to implicate him. It would be better for everyone if the thief turned out to be a stranger. It's obscene for a trusted superintendent to steal from children who love him. Do you remember what happened when the superintendent of Vinton County had an affair with one of his principals?"

Lara nodded, and Celina continued. "At first, parents were appalled. Perhaps titillated is a more accurate word. They wanted to know all the details so they could talk about how horrified they were. Then, after a week or two, the disapproval died down. People started thinking about the good things the principal and superintendent had accomplished in their work and the effort that would be involved in replacing them. Suddenly the township administrators' personal lives were nobody's business."

"The school board forced them to resign," Lara interjected.

"Yes. And then out of fear of being sued, they bought out their contracts and provided glowing letters of recommendation. The board basically said, 'You lovely people go with our blessing.'"

"What happened to them after they left Vinton?" Lara asked.

"The principal's husband divorced her. She's now teaching in a small town in Ohio. The superintendent and his wife moved out west, where he accepted a position as superintendent of a large school district, leaving the taxpayers to pick up the pieces and the financial tab for two immoral leaders who had to get out of town." Celina shook her head in disgust. "No responsibility, no consequences."

Lara eyed the Mercedes two cars in front of them. "Have you thought about how the news that Updike is a thief and a murderer will impact the children when they find out?"

Celina sighed. "The students will learn moral codes are irrelevant unless you get caught. What do you think will happen to Updike legally if we catch him?"

"People that wealthy never get the death penalty. The family money will buy him a soft bed in a luxurious prison with a golf course."

Celina followed her prey onto 1-74 East before

glancing at the clock—5:16. She picked up her cell phone and dialed her house. "Hi, honey. How are you and the twins doing? I'm going to be late tonight. You guys can call me on my cell phone if you need anything. I'll call at eight o'clock to say goodnight. Make sure they use soap in the bath. Love you too." Celina hung up. "Do you need to call anybody, Lara?"

"No. I told them I would be at my friend Patti's in Noblesville."

"Will Patti cover for you if they call there?"

"She's out of town visiting her in-laws. If she hears a strange call on her answering machine next week, I'll tell her my family must have misunderstood. By the way, Max and the kids think you're there with me. I gave them your cell phone number in case of an emergency."

"Good idea. Lara, does it ever bother you when you lie to your husband and kids about our activities?"

"I don't exactly lie," Lara denied.

"Intentionally mislead, same thing. You wouldn't accept your statements as truth if they were coming from your children to you."

"No, I wouldn't," Lara admitted, "but this isn't the same thing. FBI Detectives don't always tell their family what they're really doing either."

"We're not FBI," Celina pointed out.

"That's true. I see what we do more like a civilian secret service."

"Would you call us vigilantes?" Celina probed further.

"No! We shed light on lawbreaking, but we never execute justice ourselves. That would be going too far."

Leaving sun and city lights far behind, the two automobiles sped away from Indianapolis. Off to the side, snow laden soybean fields silently conserved their energy for spring. Occasional farmhouses broke the quilt-like patches of Indiana landscape, and billboards promised towns that were never seen from the exit. Every passing mile urged the pulse of the first car on and lulled the occupants of the second vehicle into weariness.

"Cincinnati, forty-five miles," Lara read. "Do you think he could be headed there?"

"I have no idea, but it looks like we're in for a long Friday-evening drive. Check out the CD's in the glove compartment. What kind of music would you like to hear?"

Lara reached into the glove compartment. *Piano by the Sea* sounds calming after a long day." Moments later, *Sea Time Serenade* filled the car.

"That's better. Now if we only had something to drink."

Lara reached down into her book bag and pulled out two mugs and a thermos. "I thought we might be in for a long evening. Nothing like hot mint tea on a stakeout."

"Lara, you are magnificent," Celina burst out. "You are absolutely the most prepared woman . . . or man that I have ever met."

The Sebring lagged a half mile behind its quarry, speeding up before each exit to ensure the Mercedes continued on I-74 East. The landscape changed as the highway furrowed into the rolling hills of eastern Indiana.

"I'm getting a bit drowsy," Celina admitted. "Could we change the music to something more upbeat?" In response, Lara popped in a new CD. The Temptations blasted out.

"Oh, turn up the music." Celina sang out.

> *"As pretty as you are, you know you could have
>   been a flower.*
> *If good looks were a minute, you know you could
>   have been an hour.*
> *The way you stole my heart, you know you could
>   have been a crook*
> *Baby, you're so smart, you know you could have
>   been a schoolbook."*

Lara joined the chorus with.

> *"Well you could have been anything that you
>   wanted to*
> *I can tell the way you do the things you do.*
> *I like the way you do the things you do."*

Twenty minutes and a second cup of tea later, Lara shifted her feet to get more comfortable. "I can't imagine where he's going. It's already six-thirty. If he goes much further we may need to turn around."

"We can't go home now," Celina objected. "This whole trip will have been for nothing if we don't find out what he's up to."

"The superintendent may be taking a weekend trip. I can't be gone overnight, and I doubt if you can either."

They drove on in silence. Shortly before they would have crossed the Ohio state line, they rounded a curve and saw the Mercedes' turn signal blinking.

Lara read the sign. "*Route One, Lawrenceburg. Argosy Casino.* You don't think he's going to the casino, do you?"

"Gambling? I never even thought of that."

"It would explain a desperate need for large sums of money."

"And all withdrawals ending with the lucky seventy-seven," Celina agreed. "But he puts the money back within a few days. Could he be breaking even?"

"No. Nobody breaks even a majority of the time."

"It's going to be harder to follow him without being seen on this two-lane road," Celina worried. Old-fashioned plank homes perched on the east side of the road. Front porches stuck out for the sole purpose of monitoring the traffic, much as they had done in the days of the stagecoach. To the west, cozy bungalows and expensive, custom designed log cabins snuggled down into a hillside that sloped away to the meandering Slab Camp Creek. As if in collusion with the superintendent, night doused the road in obscurity, making it even more difficult to follow the silver automobile.

"Why is he going so fast? I can hardly keep up with him." Celina complained.

"Do you think he spotted us?"

"Maybe. Or perhaps he's late for an appointment. It's six forty-five."

The road twisted and turned through an old river town where grand old mansions lined the streets. The silver Mercedes turned left and shot down a wide, open avenue. Within minutes lights loudly proclaimed the presence of Argosy Casino.

Lara shook her head as they pulled into the casino's parking garage. "So it is gambling. He must be losing his own money and replacing it with township funds."

"Why does he only steal exactly what he needs?"

"Maybe he tells himself this is the last time he'll gamble, or maybe he doesn't want his wife to know, or maybe he just needs the money there for his next gambling binge." Lara theorized.

"I've heard compulsive gambling is an addiction, like alcoholism."

"It's an illness he chooses to continue," Lara declared. "Treatment is available for those who want it."

"Well, now we have motive—desperate need for money."

"Desperate enough to kill for—twice. Let's go home," Lara announced.

"We can't go home now. We have to go in there and see what he's really up to."

"We know what he's up to—gambling. That's the only reason anyone would go to a casino."

"Not necessarily. It could be prostitution, drugs, money laundering . . ." Celina pulled into a parking spot and turned the motor off.

"Money laundering makes money. You don't have to steal to replace what you lose."

"Okay, maybe not money laundering, but we still don't know for sure it's gambling. He could be meeting a blackmailer. We need to go in."

"Celina, I am not going in a casino. That's against everything I believe in."

"You don't have to bet. We just need to make sure that he really is here to gamble. Come on. If we don't follow him now, we'll lose him. He's getting in that elevator." Celina opened the car door and jumped out.

Not willing for her friend to go alone, Lara followed.

Chapter Ten

The elevator doors reopened onto the Argosy Hotel and Casino complex. Straight ahead, carved wooden banisters surrounded the hotel's entertainment pavilion. An octagonal stained-glass map of the world arched high in the ceiling. To the left and right rich, carpeted hallways led to various theme bars and restaurants. The superintendent was nowhere in sight.

"Follow them," Celina motioned towards the patrons lining up in front of the ticket booth. The women joined the queue, trying not to gawk as they inched their way forward.

Celina craned her neck to search for the superintendent among the crowd of people pressing toward the double doors. "There are a lot of people here."

"A lot of people are going to lose a lot of money," Lara responded. "I don't see Updike. This place is huge. He could be anywhere, and we probably won't find him."

"We have to try."

They were silent for a moment as conversation between the middle-aged couple behind them caught their attention. A woman in matching lime-green polyester blouse and slacks was speaking.

"Tonight I am not going to move until my machine pays off. Last time, I put three rolls of quarters into the slot machine on the end of the aisle. I knew it was a winner. I could feel it, but you made me switch to the blackjack table. A couple of minutes later, some kid who was barely twenty-one came by and hit the jackpot with my machine. He must have won three hundred dollars."

"More like a hundred and fifty," her husband argued.

"Doesn't matter. It was my money, and that boy got it."

"Aw, you probably would have lost two hundred and fifty in the ten minutes it took the machine to pay off. Then where would you be? I did you a favor."

"Yeah, well don't do me any favors tonight."

Lara and Celina exchanged a look of amusement. A moment later, the bald man in front of them completed his transaction at the ticket booth, making it their turn to purchase admission to the lottery of luck. They hesitated, still uncertain if entering the casino would lead to finding Updike.

"How many, ma'am?" The employee's abruptness revealed a slight impatience with beginners who didn't step up to the window prepared to spit out their ticket request and move on.

"Do we have to buy tickets if we're not going to gamble?" Lara questioned.

"Yes, ma'am. You must have a ticket to board the boat."

"Boat?"

"Two tickets, please," Celina interrupted, pushing her out of the way and thrusting a twenty-dollar bill at the man. "Thank you," she grabbed the tickets and change, steering Lara towards the next line awaiting admission.

"What boat?"

"The casino is on a riverboat," Celina explained.

"We confirm he's on the boat, and we get off. Agreed?"

"As soon as we see what he's doing," Celina hedged.

In an attempt to distract Lara's attention, she pointed to the wide, grand staircase with its narrow, carpeted steps descending to the next floor. "This looks like a scene out of *Hello Dolly*. I half expect Louis Armstrong to break out in song at the bottom."

Lara glared at her.

Finally the line of players propelled them smoothly out of the movie-like setting and onto the riverboat. The moment they crossed through the double doors signifying the entrance to the floating casino the milieu changed from strategically elegant to flamboyantly gaudy. Purple and orange carpet screamed up from the floor. A thick, almost nonporous, haze stuffed cigarette smoke up their nose and into their eyes. The bald man ahead of them came to life, streaking straight towards the bar and his first drink of the night. The woman behind them raced to the end of an aisle. Pulling a tall plastic cup already labeled OUT OF ORDER from her purse, she slipped it over the arm of her favorite slot machine claiming it as her own until her husband could return with the chips. All around them, men and women jammed against each other, moving constantly, vying for a place among the crowded craps or roulette tables.

The throbbing pulse of the casino jarred their senses. It took a moment for Celina to realize the obnoxious noise heralded a discharge of tokens from the slot machines. Unmoved by their accomplishments, winners fed their prize back to the hungry machines without as much as a change of expression in their glazed eyes. "That's the same look my boys get when they sneak too much X-Box 360," Celina whispered.

Lara nodded, "Johnny, too."

Although the converted riverboat was jammed with people, many of whom had come in groups, conversation was almost nonexistent as patrons ignored each other and threw out commands like "beer," "whiskey," and "daiquiri" to demand service from women in low necklines and short skirts designed to match the carpet. Celina and Lara felt penned in, their senses on overload.

"Blend in," Celina instructed.

"You've got to be kidding," Lara retorted. "We're so out of place here, we could be part of a *Highlights* magazine picture where kids pick out what doesn't belong."

Celina ignored her. "The boat only has three floors, so he can't be too far."

"Unless he's having dinner at one of the hotel restaurants."

"If we don't find him here, we'll check the restaurants to see if he's meeting someone. I can't imagine any other reason he would come this far for dinner, especially without his wife."

"Let's find him and get out of here."

The two club members hedged their way through the roulette aisle, scanning the crowds for the superintendent. Their own discomfort at being there caught the momentary attention of casino patrons, who dismissed them with a glance. The roll of the die killed any curiosity that might have otherwise surfaced.

"Look to your left," Lara demanded. A gray-faced, elderly woman fed token after token into a slot machine, her shallow breaths aided by a small oxygen tank perched on the stool beside her. "I bet I'll be seeing her in the cardiac intensive care unit."

Celina shook her head. "When I first realized he was coming to a casino, I felt nervous. We're not dressed up, and this is definitely out of our normal environment. I was afraid I would feel outclassed or lacking in sophistication. But I don't feel intimidated at all. I feel sorry for them. Look! They're not even smiling when they win."

The two ladies pushed their way past congested gaming tables, where strategically placed mirrors reflected the toss of the ivories. Dealers called out numbers and words so fast it seemed a foreign language understood only by the players.

"There he is beside the second craps table," Lara pointed.

Stopping beside the woman whose conversation they had overheard in line, they feigned interest as she popped quarters into her lucky slot machine. Her husband stood sentinel, evidently trying to make up for past deeds by cheering her on now. From where they stood, they could observe the superintendent without drawing attention to themselves.

He watched the craps players with a detached air, interested in their strategy, but not emotionally involved in the outcome. The expression on his face remained pleasant. Only his eyes revealed an intense focus.

A break in the continuous slot machine *cha-ching* diverted their attention to the gambler beside them. "Oh, no, I'm out of quarters," the woman panicked. "I told you to get me more. Someone else is going to get my money again!"

"I'll go get you more," he promised. Then, glowering at Celina and Lara as if he suspected they were loitering nearby with the intention of stealing his wife's place at this particular slot machine, he warned, "I'll be right back."

Stunned, they looked at his wife, ready to protest any ill intent. His wife immediately flipped the Styrofoam cup upside down on the arm of the slot machine signally it was, once again, out of commission. The woman wrapped her arms around each side of the slot machine, almost in a hugging fashion, the way one might position ones self between a small child and danger. She glared at them, ready to call security if they stepped any closer to her treasure.

"Look, he's gone," Lara motioned. The empty space where the superintendent had stood had already closed up with a new surge of onlookers. The woman with her intimidating husband and imagined pot of gold were forgotten as Celina and Lara pressed through the throng of casino patrons to once again search out their quarry.

They walked to the end of the boat without any luck. They turned down a new aisle, and there he was.

The superintendent entered the sectioned off area where discreet signs announced $50 minimum bids. One or two patrons to a table, crystal chandeliers, muted decorator colors and waitresses covering more cleavage softened the ambiance and imitated a higher class. The superintendent stood still, drawing a deep breath as if savoring his return to the world of chance. His eyes roamed the high rollers corner, scrutinizing blackjack tables the way a tax auditor with a grudge painstakingly examines returns. After a brief hesitation, almost as if observing a moment of prayer, the gambler took his stance at tonight's table of choice.

"Good evening, Mr. Updike," a blackjack dealer greeted him. "Ready to take lady luck for a ride?"

"Absolutely." Updike handed a wad of money to the dealer, who counted the bills then meted out a tall stack of colored chips.

"Good luck, sir."

"Thank you," the superintendent mumbled, his thoughts already fixated.

Cards flying, the dealer dealt.

"Hit me," the gambler demanded.

With a smile, the dealer complied, laying down an eight of hearts. "Twenty-one," he congratulated.

Updike nodded his approval, as he added more chips to the winnings.

The next hand began. Host and patron moved in perfect sync. Hand after hand finished with the sole purpose of beginning the next. Sometimes the dealer won, sometimes the gambler. Nothing changed but the height of the chips.

"Looks like he's winning, but it's hard to see." Celina peered across dividers sectioning off the high rollers area. "Not to mention we look pretty stupid just standing here. I wish we could get closer to hear his conversation with the dealer, but the casino might not allow nonplayers in that section, and we would really draw attention to ourselves if they asked us to leave."

"We're already drawing attention." Lara glanced over at two security men. "They're trying to figure out why we aren't gambling."

"You're right. I know you don't want to gamble, but maybe we should for the sake of our cover," Celina suggested tentatively.

"No!"

"Not even a few quarters?"

"It's a fifty-dollar minimum in this section. Besides, it's not the amount of money involved. It's the gambling." Feeling she may have come across too strong, Lara tried to explain. "I've seen what gambling can do to people. My neighbors, Mr. and Mrs. Tibbert had been married forty-nine years when he died. She missed him horribly. Her whole life had revolved around caring for him. He left her with a good insurance policy and enough stock in Lilly Pharmaceuticals to live a comfortable, secure life. She was so lonely. Her grief overwhelmed her judgment. A couple of her widow friends convinced her to go to on a daylong casino cruise. Something in the repetition must have answered her need for constancy. A poor substitute, but still a stopgap. She went back to the casino the following Saturday, and the one after that, and the one after that. Within four months she had wiped out their entire savings, the life insurance, and three-fourths of the Lilly stock."

"Why?"

"Grief affects people in strange ways."

"What happened to Mrs. Tibbert?"

"She lives on a very fixed income. Her independence is gone. Her son monitors every penny she spends. That's why I hate gambling. It may be perfectly fine for couples that budget fifty to a hundred dollars for dining out and come to the casino, where they get free food and still not spend more than their allotted amount. But there are always innocent people who get caught up in gambling and their lives are destroyed."

"Like Richard Updike," Celina commented. Celina watched the superintendent's chiseled profile, an adrenaline rush darkening his face each time a new hand of cards was dealt.

"I don't know that I'd call him innocent, but I doubt if he started gambling with the thought that he would steal from the Township when he needed more money."

"No, I'm sure not."

Lara glanced over at the boat security. "They're still watching us, wondering why we're not playing. Perhaps we should make up a reason why we're here. Should we tell them you are a writer working on a book about gambling?"

"No." Celina pushed her friend on the elbow and turned to walk away from the men as if she had misunderstood the men's intentions and thought they were trying to pick them up. "Volunteering information without being asked would appear even more suspicious. If we say nothing, but look like housewives out for a night on the town, then they'll dismiss us as unimportant."

Lara studied Celina's face. "I believe you like having people underestimate you."

"It certainly comes in handy at times." Celina admitted. They made half a dozen turns around the boat always checking back to verify Updike was still placing bets. Discouraged by the discovery that a man so admired and trusted was a thief, Celina pointed toward the door. "We can leave now. He doesn't look like he's going anywhere for a while."

The husbands of ladies of the club were surprised when their wives offered to give them a Saturday free of family obligations if the men would then watch the children so the club members could go out for dinner in the evening. All the men agreed.

The women and their children met at Grace's mansion to prepare food for the St. Patrick's Day party. While the kids played, Lara delegated recipes, assembled ingredients, and checked off lists. Romy, whose swift movements outpaced most people, put her energy into shaping and baking shamrock cookies faster than Keebler. Celina and Tamara chopped vegetables, concocting various salads and side dishes. Grace scurried from one person to the next, pulling bowls out of cabinets, and pointing to drawers where she kept stirring utensils.

The first several hours passed swiftly with the children playing well together and the ladies making significant progress on their party preparation. About two hours before the agreed upon quitting time, Tamara's children broke out in a squabble. Amidst cries of "You're not the boss of me" and "I'm going to tell Mom," Tamara laid down her wooden stirring spoon and headed for the family room. Despite several attempts at mediation, both sides remained unforgiving and inconsolable. No, they would not compromise, and no, they could not agree to disagree and just play nicely. After several interruptions, Tamara lost patience with her children. "Debra, Keith, Julie, and Allison, each one of you in a separate chair—NOW! I am tired of the four of you squabbling. Not another word from any of you for the next fifteen minutes. For every sentence you say, I will count the words and add another minute in time out. Is that clear?" Silent nods.

Tamara reentered the kitchen, where her friends continued to work, waiting to see if she wanted to talk. She picked up her wooden spoon and beat the mixture with a vengeance. No one spoke for a minute.

Finally, Celina put one arm around her friend's shoulders. Staring into the bowl, she commented, "It's a good thing you don't practice corporal punishment on your children."

Laughter replaced the tension in the air. Tamara stopped the beating and remarked, "Sometimes I think correcting my children is the only thing I ever do."

"We've all felt like that before," Romy sympathized.

"It wouldn't be so bad if Greg didn't always come off as the good guy. He tells them yes to everything, and if they misbehave or he gets tired of them he brings them home—as if that's supposed to be a punishment. He never deals with their behavior, let alone corrects them. He does whatever it takes to come across as perfect and to make me look bad. He's not a parent, he's a buddy."

"He's a bonehead," Romy declared.

Celina hugged Tamara again. "You are a good parent, and that's what your children need. They don't need another buddy, no matter how many wishes he can grant. Your children need your parenting skills even when they resist them. Stay strong, Tamara."

"I don't feel very strong any more. I feel emotionally beaten down into nothingness."

"But you are strong, and you have to hold on to that truth."

"You're right. This mess isn't the kids' fault. They're tired of being cooped up in a tiny house. Their whole lifestyle has changed, and they don't understand why."

Perhaps the house will sell soon," Romy encouraged her. "The real estate business should be picking up now. Indianapolis doesn't have enough five-bedroom houses."

"It won't sell. He has it priced too high."

"A good realtor will tell him that, and he'll lower the price before long." Romy's heartening words fell on deaf ears.

"He won't lower the price because he doesn't want the house to sell," Tamara answered in flat tones. "The judge ruled Greg can stay in the house until it's sold, but at closing, I get half the profits as part of the settlement. By pricing it high, he ensures it won't sell, and I won't get my share of the equity."

"That's unfair," Grace fumed.

"Unfair, but legal," Tamara responded. "But then that's pretty much his motto. The kids think the divorce is my fault. The other day Greg told Keith, 'I wish we could be a happy family again. I'm very sad since Mommy took you away from me.' He insists on visitation during the week, but won't help them do their homework. Then he tells the judge I'm an inept parent because the children aren't handing in their assignments on time. He claims I am unable to provide for them adequately. I provide everything they need. I just can't afford the latest X-Box 360 game. He's decided to sue for custody. The man isn't even current on child support, but he told the judge it's because I spend it on me and the children don't get anything." Tamara's voice began to break, but she continued.

"I kept thinking that all the bad things he's done would catch up with him. They haven't. Not only does everyone still think he's Mr. Perfect, but his company is promoting him to vice-president. Can you believe it? Vice president! The man's a liar. He uses coworkers to make himself and his projects look good. He manipulates his friends, brothers, parents, even his children. Wouldn't you think somebody would eventually catch on? But it's not happening. They all act like he's wonderful. He waltzes through life damaging one person after another, and nobody objects. Nobody even notices. Or if they do, they don't say a thing. It's as if his actions don't matter as long as he's outwardly charming.

"Friends that we socialized with realize he's had affairs. They claim to be moral people, but pretend they don't want to judge. That's a lie. People love to judge. See how fast they judge when someone wrongs them." Tamara's voice imitated the way her life had shrieked out of control. "Even people at church back away from taking a stand. Sure they'll say adultery is wrong if it's an academic discussion. But most people aren't willing to confront a friend and tell him he's wrong for screwing around on his wife and children. Men who cheat on their families shouldn't be rewarded with a raise and a promotion. What's fair about that?" she spat out, rushing from the kitchen as her last ounce of reserve dissolved.

The four women remained silent for a moment, each heart aching for their friend. "This has gone on too long." Lara verbalized what they were all thinking. "Her lawyer doesn't seem to be doing anything. We need to help her."

"I suppose a hit man is out of the question," Romy muttered, wishing it wasn't. "How about if we hire Vinny the Leg Breaker?"

"You don't really know anyone called Vinny the Leg Breaker, do you?" Grace questioned. "Never mind. I don't want you to answer that."

"We couldn't hire Vinny," Celina teased. "He'd be a bad example for the children. We're trying to teach them to use their words instead of their hands when they're angry." She paused for a moment, to consider the possibility. "Actually, using our words might be exactly how we should handle this situation."

"Greg would never listen to us," Romy objected. "No matter how gregarious men like that are in public, deep within they don't respect women."

"He will if we are persuasive enough. I've negotiated business deals with men like that before. The trick is to get them to see that a particular agreement is in their own best interest. Coolidge Custom Design is a small company, isn't it?

"About a hundred employees," Lara volunteered.

"It's owned by Oscar Coolidge," Grace added. "I haven't seen Mr. and Mrs. Coolidge for a long time.

When Alex was alive, we saw them at charity functions quite often. I remember one year we sat at their table for the Five Hundred Ball. Mr. Coolidge kept our whole party in stitches with stories about his grandchildren. He and his wife are very family-oriented. They would be appalled if they knew Greg's true character."

An idea began to form in Celina's mind. "Are any of those philanthropic committees you're on currently raising money?"

"The hospital auxiliary is hosting a tour of Victorian mansions down on the Old North Side next month."

"Perfect. Could you arrange to have lunch with Mr. Coolidge to discuss his company purchasing a block of tickets?"

"Of course."

"Of course, what?" Tamara asked with a forced cheerfulness as she walked back into the room. Her face looked splotchy and emotionally drained.

"Tamara, we want to have lunch with Greg," Celina informed her.

"Why?"

"We want to reason with him. We need you to arrange a lunch meeting without telling him we'll be there. What's a good restaurant, Grace?"

"Shula's Steak House on South Capitol. Make it for a day when I'm not teaching."

Tamara closed her eyes and rubbed her temples in an effort to erase the headache. "I can't take that long of a lunch hour. Besides, he'll think I'm caving in."

"It's probably best if we talk to him alone anyway."

Tamara's eyes flew open, and she studied their faces for a moment. "You're not going to . . ." she searched for the right words and, finding none, used the first movie line that came to mind, "work him over or anything, are you?"

"We're going to reason with him." Celina reassured.

Tamara sighed. "Whatever." She felt too tired to care.

Grace raised her brows and grinned. "I don't believe anyone has ever accused me of intending to 'work someone over' before."

"I believe you could do it," Romy voiced confidence in her friend.

Chapter Eleven

Three vans, each stocked with assorted St. Patrick's Day paraphernalia and the makings of an Irish feast caravaned the winding roads crisscrossing Geist Reservoir. The vehicles pulled off Olio Road in front of the old quarry offices. A woman clothed in a crisp, hunter-green maid's uniform and white apron stepped sharply from the driver's seat to slap computer-generated emblems on the sides of the minivans, temporarily identifying them as property of Bon Appetit Catering. Back in their vans, the catering company crossed the bridge, turned right on to 113th Street, and proceeded to the Updike estate.

It took over four hours to complete set-up for the St. Patrick's Day celebration. Winking leprechauns perched precariously on bookcases and grinned playfully down from chandeliers. A hint of mint wafted up from shamrock-shaped candles and mingled with the cinnamon smell of freshly baked cookies. In every direction a guest could turn, elaborate froufrou transformed the stiff, professionally decorated rooms of the mansion into a flamboyant backdrop that invited merriment.

"How amazing!" Mrs. Updike exclaimed, clearly relieved. "All of the decorations look as if they were created specifically for these rooms. The rainbow looks perfect hanging from the upstairs balcony. How did you know the sizes?" she puzzled.

"Oh, that's what makes us the experts!" Romy avoided the question as she filled the pot of gold with chocolate nuggets and treasures. Straightening up, she invented a reason to escape further interrogation. "If you'll excuse me, I'm needed in the family room."

Round dinner tables set with service for eight were scattered throughout the mansion's main floor. In the dining room, Celina stepped back from the groaning buffet table to admire an ice sculpture of frozen flowers that she had stored in her home freezer for the past fifteen days. Too bad they couldn't have found a mold for a thirty-inch high leprechaun. That would have really looked impressive. Celina grinned, remembering the other club members' exasperation with her when she had suggested it. Romy particularly thought they were overdoing the preparations.

Glancing over, she saw her friend in the hallway. "Hey, Romy," she teased, "would you mind stitching up about a hundred dark-green chair covers within the next thirty minutes? I think it would lend that final touch of elegance to the atmosphere."

Romy entered the room and positioned a cloth leprechaun to look as if it were peeking out of an antique Silver Cross pram before answering. "No problem," she dished back. "Do you think we should make them out of real shamrocks so the guests will feel like they're standing in an Irish glen?"

"I like it," Celina admitted.

Romy glanced around the room and assessed their progress. "Everything is clean and in place," she announced. The words were barely out of her mouth before she noticed a clump of dirt on the spoke of the antique baby carriage. She whisked a cotton cloth out of her apron to catch the dirt and shine up the metal. "Now we're ready," she corrected herself. Suddenly, the realization of what she had cleaned hit her. "Celina," she whispered. "I wiped mud off the spoke of that baby carriage."

"Yes," Celina looked puzzled.

"Mud on that carriage." Romy repeated. "Where would a baby carriage, an unused, antique baby carriage get mud on the wheel?"

Comprehension hit. "Surely not!" Celina protested.

Romy nodded.

"How would Winston's body fit in there?" Celina whispered.

"It wouldn't have to fit exactly. It only needed to be propped up enough to maneuver the body around on wheels." She shook the handle, bouncing the carriage. "It has a steel frame. Look! There's a stress tear in the lining as if it's been used roughly."

"The decorations look great, ladies."

Celina and Romy looked up from the carriage to see Superintendent Updike standing beside them. "Thank you, Superintendent," Celina tried to recover. "You have such a lovely house. We were just admiring your furniture."

The superintendent nodded, looking at the carriage. "Thank you. That piece particularly is an interesting one. It's an original Silver Cross pram, made in the 1890s. They're still built in the same British town where they have always been manufactured. Many of the craftsmen today are descendents of the same people who built this one. Remarkable work. Very sturdy piece."

The two club members murmured agreement, before quickly returning to their task of preparing for the party.

The doorbell rang, announcing the first flood of invitees. Soon the main floor of the mansion filled with guests. The superintendent, genuinely delighted by the turnout, squeezed each hand with the open enthusiasm of a Baptist preacher on the first night of revival. Margaret Updike, equally relishing her role as gracious hostess, greeted each guest with a kind word, secretly smiling with pride as an occasional nosy visitor checked out the upstairs bedrooms under the guise of searching for an unoccupied restroom. Further down the spacious hall, the never idle Ms. Cole pinned green carnations on the females and presented shiny cardboard top hats to the men.

Shamrock-shaped pillows propped against sofas in the living and family rooms created a relaxed environment and encouraged guests to make themselves at home. As quickly as good manners would allow, about half of the guests meandered over to the appetizer table, where they heaped sesame seed turnovers, rarebit savories, and stuffed marinated mushrooms onto emerald-colored plates before seeking out faces they recognized. The other guests headed straight for the massive wood and leather bar searching for liquid courage to meet the demands of that oxymoron, a work social.

Tamara and Grace arrived separately. Grace mingled with teachers and administrators, passing the caterers without recognition. Tamara avoided her co-conspirators completely and concentrated on chatting with Roger and Sylvia, who had come together.

For the first two hours of the party, the Bon Appetit Catering staff barely had time to think, let alone execute their search for evidence. Appetizer plates needed to be replenished, drinks offered, and empty plates and cups continuously picked up from tables, shelves, and the lid of the grand piano.

Recognizing there was no way to entirely avoid the possibility a guest might recognize one of them, the caterers tried, nevertheless, to avoid drawing attention to themselves. Staying securely in the background and never speaking unless first spoken to, Celina, Romy, and Lara experienced the sense of invisibility and nonentity that comes to America's hired serving class.

Celina felt an imperious tap on her elbow as she retrieved two half-filled glasses hidden behind a potted philodendron. Straightening up, she faced a sharp-featured librarian who peered at her with the disapproval bestowed on children who did not return borrowed books on time. "Yes, ma'am?" Celina inquired.

"I'd like a bit more of that dip," the woman demanded. Celina's eyes widened at the woman's general-like tone. As Vice-president of Training and Development for a major corporation, Celina was used to being the one in charge. People spoke to her with respect, and she addressed everyone in the company with the same level of courtesy and high regard. Fire in her eyes, she hesitated for a moment. Then remembering her role for the evening she smiled and offered the tray of Sicilian cheese and bagel chips she was holding.

"This is almost as good as the Sicilian cheese from Keystone at the Crossing's Cheese Shoppe," the woman informed her.

Celina bit back a smile as she pictured the Keystone at the Crossing container from which she had transferred the cheese before leaving home. "It is as good as the Cheese Shoppe," she asserted gently.

"Not quite, but almost," the librarian corrected.

"Would you help me replenish these trays?" Lara intervened before Celina could respond.

"How's it going?" Lara whispered once they were safe behind kitchen doors.

"I never noticed how rude people are to waitresses," Celina protested. "Would you believe one man actually dropped his napkin on the floor, bent halfway down to retrieve it, then saw me, straightened back up, and motioned for me to pick it up for him! How can people treat other human beings like that? We may be the hired help, but we weren't paid for at the auction."

"You've obviously never been a server before," Lara observed, then switched the discussion to their real concern. "Have you had a chance to search for evidence Updike is stealing administration funds to finance his gambling habit?"

"These people are keeping me so busy I haven't even been near his study. Romy and I think we discovered the baby carriage he used to transport Winston's body to the trail." Celina filled Lara in on their theory of the Silver Cross pram.

Worry lines crossed Lara's forehead. "He showed up right as you were talking about it? Do you have any idea how much he heard?"

Celina shook her head. "He may have heard everything or paid attention to nothing."

"Well, be careful. Where's Romy now?"

"Right here," Romy answered, joining them and dumping a tray full of empty dishes on the kitchen counter. "The buffet table is amply supplied and the wet bar is restocked, so perhaps we can get in a few minutes of searching before the guests finish dinner."

Lara paused as the door opened, and Tamara slipped through to join them. "Mrs. Updike keeps this house so organized; all his papers must be in a logical place. Tamara, do you want to do another search of his study, specifically the computer files?"

"I do. It's possible he might have stored something of interest on a floppy disc. That wouldn't have shown up when Romy did a remote search of his computer files."

"I pray you find it," Celina murmured.

"Don't you think it's a bit odd to ask the Almighty to assist you in snooping?" Lara questioned.

"Not at all," Celina defended her theology. "The Lord works in mysterious ways, and I want to help Him."

"I won't touch that comment," Lara responded. "We better check out the basement as well. Celina, why don't you do that?"

Celina shuddered at the memory of her last visit. "At least we know Winston's not in the closet this time."

"Updike could be storing a different body there now," Romy teased. The dread on Celina's face made her feel a shade guilty. "Sorry. I'll come with you. The basement's so big it will probably take both of us to check it out."

The four women separated. Lara detoured past Grace's table, pushing her glasses far up on her nose, a signal that they were ready to begin the search. Grace engaged the superintendent in a discussion of whether or not he thought the township should add additional full day kindergarten classes to accommodate the growing number of mothers working outside the home.

Standing by the kitchen door, Lara kept an eye open

for guests that needed assistance and club members who needed backup. She allowed herself a small sigh of relief when Celina and Romy disappeared down the stairs without being noticed.

Tamara slipped into the superintendent's study and closed the door. Glancing past the open blinds, she pulled a pair of Grace-supplied sterilized gloves out of her pocket and slipped them on.

Tamara twirled the rod, closing the blinds. Hopefully, no one was out in the yard looking inside. Opening the black file box, she flipped through the discs, assessing each label for its possible value: none claimed any contents but the same software startup and laser printer discs they had on her last visit. Snapping the lid shut, she moved the box back into place beside the computer.

Where might she find evidence of his theft? For that matter, what would proof look like? It didn't seem likely that a man this sly would leave documentation of his dishonesty just lying around for his wife or anyone else to find. What would his wife think if she knew the man she adored, trusted, and respected, not only had a serious gambling problem, but was also stealing money from the children of the township, theirs included, to finance his weakness?

Tamara eased open the thin center drawer of his desk to discover a row of gold Cross pens and corresponding mechanical pencils. The upper left hand drawer contained neatly stacked blue embossed stationary in assorted sizes. The lower left drawer offered hanging files.

"Hmm, this might be interesting," Tamara speculated. Bending down she read the neatly typed color-coded labels: Charities; Correspondence; Finances-Personal; Republican Party; Retirement; Seminars; Vacation Ideas.

She slipped the Finances-Personal folder out of the file. Even before she opened it, computer generated slips fluttered to the floor. Scooping them up, she scrutinized each one individually. These were the withdrawal slips issued every time he went on a gambling spree. The numbers and dates were the same as the records Romy had retrieved from the bank. The withdrawals weren't evidence because the numbers didn't correspond exactly with the missing amounts. That was always in nice, round, even numbers. Tamara frowned as she stared at the papers. Uneasiness nagged at her mind, almost as if she should be seeing something, but wasn't, as if she should notice something was missing. What was it? She studied the withdrawal slips closely. Everything appeared to be filled out correctly.

So deep was she in thought that Tamara barely heard Lara's voice carry down the hall. "Mrs. Updike, may I have a word with you?"

Tamara froze.

"Certainly. What can I do for you?" In contrast to Lara's overly loud speech, Margaret Updike's modulated voice sounded muffled. Tamara thrust the receipts back into their folder and shoved the drawer shut.

"I need to speak with you about dessert." Lara continued in loud strains.

"Yes?"

"When would you like it served?"

"At ten o'clock, just as we discussed earlier."

"That's right. Would you mind coming to the kitchen and taking a look at the desserts?" Lara persisted.

"Why? Is there a problem?" Mrs. Updike questioned the caterer.

"Not . . . exactly. I just thought it would be a good idea for you to look them over before we open the dessert buffet."

"Very well. I will meet you there shortly."

"I wish you would come right now. It's almost ten o'clock."

"I will meet you there in a moment," Mrs. Updike repeated, her voice taking on a slightly annoyed edge. "First I need to get a book from the study that my husband wants to lend to one of the teachers." Her voice softened to its usual pleasant tones. "I'm sure everything is perfect. Give me two minutes, and I'll be with you."

Anne Klein shoes tapped against the polished wood floor, signaling the hostess' approach. Alarmed to action, Tamara glanced around the room for a hiding place. The closet! She hesitated for the briefest moment. The last time one of them had opened a closet in this house, a dead body fell out. Unfortunately no alternative presented itself. Blinds do not provide the hiding space floor-length curtains provide in mystery novels, and the desk sides didn't go all the way to the floor. A person entering the room could immediately see anyone crouching behind it. Tamara darted for the closet.

She didn't get the closet door entirely shut before the outside knob to the study turned, and Mrs. Updike entered. Tamara stood stagnant, uncertain what to do. Even if she closed the door without a sound, the movement was sure to attract attention. If she left it ajar, the untidiness might be equally obvious to the fastidious woman. Tamara decided to take a chance the woman would be in too much of a hurry to get back to her guests to wonder why it was open.

The footsteps halted as Margaret paused to locate the book she had come to collect. The upside of the door being slightly ajar was that, by peering through the crack between door and frame, Tamara was able to watch the hostess' reflection in the mirror.

Suddenly the woman's eyes focused on the slightly open door. She swung around. Tamara held her breath as the woman zeroed in on the disarray. "Honestly," the superintendent's wife fussed, "why can't that husband of mine ever shut a door after he opens it!" Obviously irritated, Margaret slammed the door with more force than was necessary, shutting Tamara into a sightless, but relief-filled enclosure. The club member smiled and for the first time in her life, thanked God for man's inability to close the doors he opens.

A discreet ten minutes later, Tamara met Romy in the hallway. "Any luck?" Romy whispered.

"Yes," Tamara acknowledged. "But I didn't find any proof."

"What did you find?"

"Withdrawal slips for his Friday evening adventures."

"Nothing illegal about that."

"Tamara!" Richard Updike advanced toward them. "The dancing's going to start in a few minutes. Are you ready to kick up your heels?"

"Oh, I'm not sure I'll dance." Tamara tried to think up an excuse. "Irish step dancing has pretty intricate steps."

"You'll do fine. Nobody here tonight will be expert enough to know if you're missing a step. They'll be impressed you're out there giving it a whirl. Promise you'll dance a round with me."

Tamara gave him a look she intended to be noncommittal, but which he took as agreement.

"Great!" he enthused and set off to recruit more dance partners for the evening.

Tamara and Romy were about to resume their conversation when Mrs. Updike turned the corner of the hallway. "Oh, there you are, Romy. Everyone has been through the dessert line once. You can start refilling the serving trays, so they still look appetizing. I asked the band to start playing again."

"Yes, ma'am. We won't let any of the platters look bare."

Mrs. Updike smiled at Tamara. "Was there something you needed from the caterers, Tamara?"

"No, I, ah, just wanted to compliment them on the food. It's delicious."

"I agree they've done a marvelous job, and I'm so pleased you enjoyed it. Would you mind helping me interest the other guests in a little round dancing?"

"The superintendent's enthusiasm alone should have

everyone stomping their feet in no time," Tamara laughed.

The hostess slipped her arm through Tamara's. "My husband swears he has mastered a six-hand reel and is determined to perform it tonight. It was all I could do to prevent him from buying the shoulder sash, kilt, and knee socks."

Tamara laughed. "People might be willing to pay to see that. We could use it as a fund-raiser."

"That is exactly what I am afraid will happen," his wife admitted as strains of a four-piece band's Irish jig induced toes to tapping and minds to carousing.

A nimble touch on the accordion and the cry of a fiddle lured well-fed guests to the family room as the band struck up an exuberant Irish song. Silver flute and laughter doused the night with gaiety, transforming the tapping of toes into hilarious attempts at set dancing. Overstuffed sofas and soft leather chairs were pushed back against the draperies to make room for the four couples squaring up to stumble and shriek their way through the steps.

The ever-personable Richard Updike led the merriment, encouraging all but the seriously shy to venture a figure or two. Guests crowded into the corners of the room joined the frolic, clapping wildly whenever a brave reveler broke out in a solo jig.

"Now it's your turn," the superintendent insisted. Taking Tamara by the hand, he led his latest partner into position. With gentle pushes and shoves, he guided her through the movements, making both of them look as if they knew what they were doing. His agility and

strength surprised her. Although she had always known
he was in good physical condition, the business suits he
wore hid the extent of his athleticism. Halfway through
the dance, Tamara forgot about feeling self-conscious
and threw herself into the moment, matching her partner motion for motion.

When the music ended, the superintendent gallantly
bowed his gratitude for the dance. Laughing, Tamara
bobbed a curtsy. Mr. Updike couldn't possibly be a
murderer. They must have misread a clue or bungled
the reasoning. Even the gambling must be a misunder-
standing. After all, Celina and Lara had only stayed
long enough to see him play a couple hands of cards.
They did not physically see him lose thousands of dollars. For all they know, he may have left the casino
shortly after they did. The people of the township and
their children meant too much to him. He would never
steal from them. Tomorrow she would talk to the other
club members and convince them to rethink their rationale. There had to be another explanation.

Warmed by the dance and an illusory moment of con-
tentment, Tamara searched the room to check on her
partners. Romy had positioned herself near the door so
she could scoop up discarded half-empty cups of punch
before they spilled on the carpet or made rings on the piano's black finish. Celina offered the guests fresh drinks.
Grace chatted with a circle of teachers and administrators. Lara was out of sight, probably in the kitchen.

Tamara's eyes fastened on Amy Cole. The woman's
face stared back, rigid with fanatic possessiveness. Evi-

dently, not everyone had enjoyed watching Tamara and the superintendent dance. The administrative assistant burned with anger. The sight reminded Tamara of a fairy-tale illustration where the princess angered the little man by guessing the name Rumplestilskin. Tamara believed that had they not been in public, the administrative assistant would have literally stomped up and down. Disquieted by the mental tantrum, Tamara turned away.

The twang of a banjo summoned guests to the next dance. Sylvia grabbed Roger's hand for a reel. Neither one could dance, but the receptionist refused to be left out of the fun. Her feet clunked out a rhythm inconsistent with the song's beat, but fairly repetitive in its own pattern. Roger, a partner more by room position than by actual movement, did his best to appear invisible, grinning sheepishly at anyone who managed to catch his eye.

Tamara smiled, delighted to see Grace partner with a male teacher. Her friend still had not resumed dating since her husband's death two years before. Grace had always loved dancing. During her marriage, the southern belle had won the hearts of Orthodox matrons by mastering the intricate steps of Greek folk dance. A flair for mimicking choreography was second nature to her light feet, and these Irish jigs were no exception. Glancing around for her friends, Tamara saw by their smiles that each had noticed Grace dancing and were rejoicing that she had taken another step away from grief.

The moment their dance was over, Roger disappeared through the crowd. Laughing, Sylvia followed, determined to coerce him into one more dance. Their space on the floor was quickly filled by guests previously too shy to join in, who were now convinced they couldn't possibly look as bad as Roger.

"It's so hot in here. Somebody, open a window," an exhausted voice demanded. The window screeched its protest at the unseasonable request, but an icy breeze swept off the frozen reservoir, reviving the dancers.

The music changed, filling the air with *The Cliffs of Dooneen*.

> *"You may travel far, far from your own native home,*
> *Far away o'er the mountains, far away o'er the*
> *foam,*
> *But of all the fine places that I've ever been,*
> *There is none can compare with the cliffs of*
> *Dooneen."*

A change in music tempo shifted the evening's pace. A less-formal air permeated the lengthening celebration. Guests relaxed, snuggling a little closer to their escorts. Loud joking and shouts subsided. Conversation melted into a subdued prattle that blended into the party background. A few partiers, two or three in their cups, sang along, murmuring the words half a beat behind the ballad. The song ended, the clapping died away, and an Irish tenor began to croon.

> *"Oh Danny boy, the pipes, the pipes are calling*
> *From glen to glen, and down the mountain side*

The summer's gone, and all the roses falling
'Tis you, 'tis you must go, and I must bide."

Superintendent Updike wedged himself in between Tamara and another guest. "Are you having a good time, Tamara?"

At the sound of his voice, Tamara felt a twinge of guilt. Like a habitually fast driver instinctively checks the speedometer every time he passes a police car, she glanced over to see Ms. Cole's reaction. Tamara breathed a sigh of relief. No metaphorical red light in the rearview mirror. In other words, the administrative assistant was nowhere to be seen.

"I am," Tamara answered. "This is a lovely party. You and Mrs. Updike always make people feel so welcome in your home."

Mr. Updike leaned his head closer to her ear. "Glad to hear you're enjoying it. The evening has turned out rather well, hasn't it? I can't take any of the credit. Margaret is a whiz at planning these events. She keeps everything around this place running on an even keel."

Tamara smiled, and the tenor crooned on.

"But come you back when summer's in the meadow
Or when the valley's hushed and white with snow
'Tis I'll be there in sunshine or in shadow
Oh Danny boy, oh Danny boy, I love you so."

How incredible to be so loved by a man. Richard Updike obviously worshiped his wife. Margaret adored him as well. Tamara's heart ached as she thought of her own failed marriage.

"But if you come, and all the flowers are dying
And if I am dead, as dead I may well be
You'll come and find the place where I am lying
And kneel and say an "Ave" there for me.
And I shall hear, tho' soft you tread above me."

A cry broke the melody like a minstrel off key.

"What was that noise?" a guest asked.

"Sounded like a dog in pain," another answered.

Tamara glanced up to gauge the superintendent's reaction to the noise and realized the yelp came from him. His eyes stared straight ahead. Bright red seeped down his head and face.

Chapter Twelve

Undaunted by what he thought to be an intoxicated guest, the tenor continued to serenade.

"And all my dreams shall warm and sweeter be
If you will bend and tell me that you love me
Then I will sleep in peace until you come to me."

"Sit down," Tamara instructed. Maternal instinct took over, and she pushed the mute superintendent into a chair. "You're going to be alright," she told him, not having any idea whether or not her promise was true. "We're going to get you some help. Do you understand what I'm saying?"

He caught his breath, mentally swallowing the sting. His eyes turned to her in disbelief. Unable to articulate his shock, he nodded acknowledgement.

Tamara examined the blood flowing from his head. She couldn't tell how badly he was hurt, but knew they had to stop the bleeding. He winced as she gently pressed her hand flat against the side of his head. "We need an ambulance," she announced to the teacher beside her.

"I'll call 911," a woman volunteered.

"They're calling an ambulance," a man's booming voice announced to the crowd in general. His words carried across the room with a vague realization that something horrible had happened. The band stopped playing. Chaos replaced the music. A muddle of voices attempted to generate order but only heightened the disruption.

"What's happening? There's too much noise around this place," the librarian complained.

"We need quiet," the woman on the phone pleaded. "Everyone, please be quiet. I'm trying to talk to the police." The noise level increased as additional guests joined the commotion, each one hushing the other.

"He's bleeding," was the next phrase repeated through out the room. But no one knew who said it or who was bleeding.

Lara heard the comment. Her professional training kicked in, and she moved to assist.

"Wait!" Romy commanded, pulling her back. "You're a caterer."

"Someone has been hurt," Lara protested.

"Wait to see if you're needed," Romy insisted.

Lara kept silent, but maneuvered herself closer to the group encircling the superintendent.

Mrs. Updike progressed through the feverish crowd

calming guests as she moved. "Don't worry. Everything's fine. It sounds as if a woman simply fainted, probably from the excitement and the stuffiness of the room. We're a bit overcrowded in here." Margaret, always a model of cool composure, glided through the swarm to reach the center of turbulence where her husband sat in disbelief, stunned more by the fact that anyone would want to hurt him than from the pain itself.

Her face went from placid to horror at the realization the disturbance had been caused not by a fainted guest, but by her husband who had been harmed. The sight of blood covering the side of his head dissolved her self-control. "Richard," she gasped. "Not you!"

His wife's fear caused him to snap out of his shock. "I'm alright, Maggie."

"Is anyone here a medical doctor?" Celina called out as more guests attempted to surge in from adjoining rooms.

"Helen's husband is a doctor," Grace volunteered a fellow teacher's spouse.

"I'll find him," a voice responded.

"Do you have any blankets we can use to keep him warm, Mrs. Updike?" Lara asked, taking charge.

"Blankets?" the hostess repeated as if unable to comprehend the object.

"Blankets," Lara repeated. It irritated her when intelligent, seemingly well-adjusted people fell apart during a crisis. "We need blankets to keep him warm and stop shock from setting in."

Margaret remained stagnant.

"I'll get them," the voice of the administrative assistant asserted itself. In less than a minute Ms. Cole returned, laden with three blankets each made of one hundred percent lambs wool.

Lara assessed the wound. It looked like a bullet had grazed the side of his head. She began to dab away the excess blood and apply pressure to the wound.

A silver-haired man in his late fifties pushed his way through the crowd and identified himself as Dr. Maddox. "Are you a nurse?" the doctor questioned.

Startled, Lara yanked her hands away from the wound. "Caterer."

"You would have made a good nurse." Dr. Maddox pronounced, as he leaned forward to examine the superintendent. "I'll need my medical bag. It's in the car, a black Mercedes. License plate DRMAD. I parked to the left of the basketball court."

"I'll get it for you, Doctor," Roger volunteered.

"I'm coming with you," Sylvia insisted.

Dr. Maddox tossed his keys to the accountant before kneeling to examine the superintendent. "Let's take a look at what we've got here. You . . ." he indicated Lara, "hold his head still, so I can take a look at it. Good. The bullet skimmed the side of his forehead. There's always a lot of bleeding associated with head wounds."

The last of Margaret's confident persona dissolved. "How could this happen? You were just standing there listening to the band."

"Please take Mrs. Updike to the other room," the doctor demanded.

"No! I can't leave him!"

Tamara intervened. "Mrs. Updike, why don't we go upstairs and pack a few items he'll need for the hospital."

Two sirens screamed in the distance. "Those cars out there need to be moved out of the driveway, so the ambulance can get through," the doctor barked. Several guests responded to his command.

"Where the devil is my bag? I need to get this blasted bleeding stopped!" the doctor thundered.

Roger rushed into the room out of breath. "Here it is!" he thrust the medical bag at the waiting physician.

A few minutes later, footsteps pounded on the entry marble floor as paramedics stomped their way into the mansion, banging the metal sides of the stretcher against custom woodwork.

"In here! In here!" several voices added confusion to the chaos. The doctor's voice rose above the jumbled noises to direct the emergency workers to his patient.

Unable to keep silent, Lara issued a command. "Would everyone please clear out of this room and allow the doctor space to work."

Reluctant to miss the action, the guests hesitated, backed out of the room, then reconvened in the hallways and library to rehash the shooting with personal tales of where each had stood and almost been wounded by the bullet.

"I was standing not two feet away."

"I was less than that."

"Some crazy person must be trying to kill everyone

who works at the administrative office. That's the third one."

"Surely none of these incidents are related," a principal protested.

"How can you think they are not?" a teacher replied.

"I was talking to Superintendent Updike just a minute before the shooting, asking him what he thinks of the new principal at Forest Dale Elementary. Had the conversation been any longer, I wouldn't be standing here to tell about it. Imagine that!"

From five different vantage points, the ladies of the club witnessed the guests' reactions to the shooting. When possible, they engaged guests in conversation, hoping to learn details that might prove helpful when they had time to assemble the facts.

All of their secrets might come out now—beginning with the whole catering charade. They lingered in the background preparing for their opportunity to escape. Celina made the rounds of the downstairs, tossing discarded cups and retrieving empty dishes. Romy zipped around the kitchen, packing items up, stacking the dishwasher. Lara hovered near the doctor, her professional ethics not allowing her to stray from where her training might be required.

The bleeding was controlled, and Updike's voice could be heard protesting the trip to the hospital. "No need for Margaret and me to spend hours in a waiting room while physicians treat patients with real emergencies. You can bandage me up, Doctor."

Dr. Maddox glanced at the superintendent with new appreciation. It was nice to see a patient not overreacting. "You need a CAT scan to make sure the impact of the bullet didn't crack your skull. If everything looks good, which I think it will, then you can come back home tomorrow morning."

"What about the gun report?" A serious looking paramedic with a wrestler's build directed his question to the physician.

"I'll take care of that," Sergeant Detective Crooke spoke from the doorway.

"Gun report!" the superintendent exclaimed. "Is that really necessary?"

"It is required by law," Detective Crooke's six-foot-two frame towered in the doorway, with Detective Hubbard behind him.

"I didn't know the police had been called," Richard commented.

"911 received a call that there had been a shooting. Any time there's a shooting they automatically dispatch an ambulance, the fire department, and the police. Are you able to tell me what happened, sir?"

"I don't really know. I was standing right here enjoying the music. The next thing I knew I felt this searing hot pain across the side of my head. I looked down and saw blood dripping on my shirt."

"Do you have any idea who might have shot you?"

"No. The room was swamped with people. Guess it was someone who didn't like my attempt at Irish dancing." Not even Ms. Cole smiled at this attempt at humor.

"Who else was around you?"

"Staff members, the band, a principal from Lake Forest Junior High, and the physics teacher from Lincoln High. I don't recall anyone else in particular."

"Excuse me, Detective," Ms. Cole appeared at his side. "Amy Cole. You recall I am Superintendent Updike's administrative assistant. Some of the guests are trying to leave." She pronounced the word *guests* as if they were suspects. "Would you like for me to stop them?"

Detective Crooke marveled that such a small body could stop close to a hundred guests from mass exiting, but judged from her demeanor that she probably could. "If you wouldn't mind, it would be helpful. Someone may have seen something."

"How would you like them organized?" Ms. Cole asked, a determined glint lighting her eye.

The thought crossed his mind to suggest alphabetically by their mother's maiden name, but he was half afraid the administrative assistant might accomplish it. "According to the room they were in would be fine. Detective Hubbard can begin taking statements."

Ms. Cole nodded once and darted out of the room to perform her assignment. Detective Hubbard followed at a slower pace.

Celina stuck her head into the room. "Doctor, if you're finished with the superintendent, a lady in the dining room is rather upset. Perhaps you could speak with her. She mentioned she has high blood pressure and is concerned that the shooting might bring on a heart attack." Celina's smile and half-apologetic tones soothed the doctor's ire at having to deal with a hysterical guest who was not even in the room at the time of the shooting.

Detective Crooke turned back to the superintendent. "Did you hear any unusual noise at the time of the shooting, perhaps the sound of breaking glass?"

"No," the superintendent looked surprised. "But then the band was so loud, and we were standing right beside it. I could hardly hear Tamara speaking."

"Tamara?"

"One of my accountants, very proficient with the numbers. I believe you met her at the office when you were investigating Winston's death."

"Ah, Ms. Montgomery. I remember. Yes, I would like to have a word with her."

Tamara stepped out from behind the grand piano where she had tried to remain inconspicuous. "Good evening, Detective Crooke."

"Well, well, Ms. Montgomery. What a surprise to see you here tonight."

"All of the township administrative personnel are required to attend," Tamara shot back. Immediately she regretted satisfying the man with such a defensive response.

"You don't mind answering a few questions for me, do you?"

"Of course not," she lied.

"Did you notice anything unusual tonight?"

"Nothing." She was honestly perplexed. "As the superintendent said, we were standing there listening to the band sing *O Danny Boy*. I complimented him on how well the party was going. I was looking at the band when he cried out. At first, I wasn't sure who had been hurt. It was noisy in here and, of course, everyone was engrossed in the music. The band kept playing. Blood was dripping down the side of his head. I realized that it was a gunshot wound."

"And you knew what a gunshot looked like?" he queried.

Tamara hesitated. The gunshot wounds she had seen were all related to club's "extracurricular" activities, but there was no police record of her having been involved with a shooting. If she admitted to having seen one, he would push her for details, taking her down paths toward past events she would definitely prefer to avoid. Best to keep it simple. "Movies."

"Really? I wouldn't have thought you were the type of woman who enjoyed graphic violence in her choice of movies."

Tamara looked at him with an expression she hoped implied innocence. He paused for a moment, and then continued, "Did you see anyone here who should not have been at the party?"

"I don't know all of the guests. I'm not sure anyone here does. My understanding is the party was for the administrative staff and some of the teachers and principals who have township responsibilities. It is basically a thank you from the Updikes to township staff."

Although shooed out earlier while the doctor was still working on the superintendent, Roger reappeared at the doorway. Dressed in a heavy blue jean jacket lined with sheepskin, he entered the room. A look of grim determination replaced his normally cheerful expression. His presence interrupted the interview, but he waited for Detective Crooke to acknowledge him before speaking.

Sylvia hovered at Roger's shoulder. Melted wet flakes of snow slid down her neck. She shivered and pulled her thick, red, winter cape closer, her hand pushing on Roger's elbow as if to propel him forward. Uncharacteristically nervous, she fiddled with the collar on her cape, and then opened her mouth to speak.

Before any sounds were uttered, Roger spoke. He made his announcement apologetically in the tone of one about to communicate bad news. "Sir, Sylvia and I need to speak with you a moment."

Detective Crooke nodded. "Roger, isn't it? You're an accountant from the administration office?"

"Yes. There's something you might want to see. It . . ." Here he faltered and looked around at the crowd as if unsure how much information to share in front of others, "might be evidence."

"Let's take a look," Detective Crooke suggested.

"We went outside because the doctor needed his black bag out of his Mercedes," Roger began.

"Lots of people went out to move their cars for the ambulance," Sylvia interjected.

Roger nodded and then pulled a sleek piece of black metal from his pocket. "It was discarded in a pile of snow. We found it on our way back in."

Detective Crooke glanced at the handgun, but made

no move to take it. His focus remained intent on the two employees claiming to have found the evidence. "Were you looking for the gun?"

"No, not at all," Sylvia spoke up. "We had nothing to do with any of this. Roger almost tripped over something. He picked it up to see what it was. I realized it was a gun, grabbed it away, and threw it back down on the snow."

"Why did you throw it back down after you had picked it up?" Detective Crooke asked in a quiet voice.

"It was a gun—evidence. Naturally the police would need to know exactly where it was found. Besides, I hate guns. They can go off accidentally. You read about that kind of thing happening all the time."

Detective Crooke pulled out his handkerchief, casually reaching over to take possession of the gun. "Then what happened?"

"I picked it back up, sir. I didn't think a gun, most likely a loaded gun, should be left unattended. I marked the spot where we found it, but I doubt if that will tell you anything. It was too far away from the house for someone to have thrown it out a window. All of the snow from the front door to the drive has been trampled on. You can see individual shoe prints in the snow, but that could be any number of guests. We were told to move our cars out of the ambulance's way."

"Did you happen to see anyone drop anything, stoop to pick something up or even fall while you were out here moving your cars?"

"No," Sylvia denied almost as quickly as he asked.

Roger shook his head. "I really wasn't paying any attention to anybody else."

"Where were you parked, and where is your car now?"

"It was parked up here by the lamp post before the shooting. We pulled up on the lawn because there wasn't enough space on the street," Roger explained. "I drive a Volkswagen Rabbit. It's out past the fishing pond now. I hope we don't get stuck. It's snowing again."

"Where was your car?" Detective Crooke addressed Sylvia.

"Mine? I didn't drive. I came with Roger."

"Then why did you come outside to move the car?"

"I wanted an excuse to get out of the house." When this reasoning was met with silence, she continued her explanation. "Someone had just shot the superintendent. The gunman may still have been in the house. I didn't want to be in there if he went on a shooting rampage. We already had two people in our office die. I don't want to be another victim."

"What makes you think the three are connected?"

Sylvia looked at the policeman with the contempt she reserved for those who treated middle-aged women as if they had lost their capacity for logic. "I am fifty-four years old, Detective, near retirement, but hardly senile. It is unlikely that the stabbing death of Mr. Dopplar, the suicide of Ms. Patterson, and the attempted homicide of the superintendent, all three from the same office, could be anything but connected."

"My apologies, ma'am." His voice was respectfully

low with remorse. "I thought perhaps you might have noticed something I missed."

She withered him with a look that clearly communicated she thought he might be suffering from a bit of early senility himself to try flattery on her. "You're either lying or you think I may be the gunman."

Detective Crooke shrugged his shoulders and smiled. "We must consider all the possibilities, mustn't we?"

Sylvia's eyes widened for a moment before she returned his smile. She had intended to shock the policeman into treating her respectfully as a possible witness, not a real suspect. "My fingerprints are on the gun."

"You mentioned you picked it up. You are the receptionist, if I remember correctly."

"That's right."

"You see the comings and goings at the administration office."

"All day, every day," she confirmed.

"So what's your theory?"

She studied his face, trying to determine whether or not he really wanted to hear her opinion.

"Everyone has a theory," he coaxed.

"I think it must be a disgruntled employee."

"What might that employee be disgruntled about?"

"Failure to receive a raise or promotion."

"I don't know anyone who is that disgruntled," Roger objected. "School employees don't go around shooting and stabbing people because they were denied a raise or promotion. We're not a bunch of wacked-out postal employees."

"What do township employees do when they don't receive the raise or promotion they believe they deserve?" Detective Crooke addressed him.

"They come in late, take extended breaks, use up all their sick time or even waste time without accomplishing anything, but they don't kill people. The real question is why would a killer choose an accountant, a data processing clerk, and a superintendent? What would they have in common?"

"Good question," Detective Crooke approved. "Do you see any connection?"

"None. Winston and the superintendent are management, but Cindy was an hourly clerk."

A crowd had reconvened around the superintendent forming a semicircle, like reporters after a breaking news story. Ms. Cole returned and took up her post as sentry, glaring at any guest who dared look less than awed with her boss's bravery.

"Do you recognize this?" Detective Crooke leaned over so the superintendent could see the .38 caliber revolver cradled in his handkerchief.

"That looks like my wife's gun!" the superintendent exclaimed.

Chapter Thirteen

"Where does your wife normally keep her gun?" Detective Crooke asked.

"In a locked cabinet in the master bedroom closet when she's home. If she's attending one of her charity committee meetings downtown and it's going to be a late night, she carries it in her purse."

"Does she keep bullets in it?"

"No, of course not. We have children. The bullets are kept at the back of my nightstand."

"Who had access to the upstairs?"

"Everyone," a voice answered for him.

Detective Crooke looked up to see Amy Cole standing with her back against the wall. The administrative assistant continued, "People have been going up and down those stairs all night. Anyone at the party could have stolen the gun."

"Including you?" he baited her.

"Yes," she replied without flinching, "including me."

Now here, he thought, is a woman ready to throw herself on the sacrificial altar for the man of her choice.

"And did you?" he continued.

"No." She sighed, evidently regretting her inability to take this responsibility off the superintendent's shoulders.

"Who do think might have a reason to kill the superintendent?"

"No one," the angry little head bobbed sideways in fury.

"Someone did," Detective Crooke corrected, watching as the paramedics left with the superintendent.

The next hour stretched itself unmercifully as guests waited to give their statements. Few of them had little of value to tell, but most were impatient to share it. One woman swore she had heard glass breaking, but an examination of the bullet's flight pattern revealed it must have entered through the open window.

Detective Crooke noted the bullet's line of flight from the window to where it pierced the paneling, struck a stud and dropped down between the drywall. He pulled Roger aside. "Why was the window open in March?"

"The room was crowded. People were hot from dancing. Someone wanted the window open so we could breathe easier."

"Who suggested opening the window?"

Roger shook his head. "I have no idea."

Sylvia shivered. "It's late. You have my statement. May I go home now?"

"Certainly," he agreed. "I can call you at the office if necessary." He handed each of them his card. "If you think of anything that might be helpful, I'd appreciate hearing from you."

Roger and Sylvia left quickly, their exit scrutinized by a watchful Ms. Cole.

Detective Crooke handed the revolver over to Detective Hubbard with instructions to mark and bag the evidence. He then turned his attention to searching for more clues.

"I believe I'll take a look around to see if anything seems unusual or out of place." He began his inspection at the top of the mansion, working his way down to the basement. The place looked remarkably in order for a home that had just hosted a large party.

The five club members congregated in the kitchen for a stolen huddle. "What are we going to do?" Romy whispered.

"We're going to keep him away from the real Mrs. Updike. That's what we're going to do," Tamara's voice shook. "If he realizes Grace is not the real Mrs. Updike, he'll question the alarm the night of our tea party. The whole mess will unravel and all five of us will end up in jail."

"I'll keep him away from her," Romy declared.

Lara studied the determined expression on Romy's face. "Perhaps Celina should be the one to keep Mrs. Updike out of sight. Why don't you help me clean this place up so we can get out of here as soon as he re-leases us?"

"Releases us," Tamara repeated. "It sounds like we've already been thrown in jail."

At that moment, Detective Hubbard entered the kitchen. Talking immediately ceased. "Excuse me," Tamara muttered. She and Celina ducked out the door.

"Good evening, Mrs. Updike," the officer addressed Grace.

"Good evening, Detective," Grace pushed a golden curl behind her ear, revealing her nervousness at playing hostess while the real Mrs. Updike was only a room or two away.

"This has been a difficult night for you. Are you doing alright?"

"Yes, thank you." It required no effort for Grace to make her voice sound distraught.

"Do you think the shooting tonight might be connected to the break-in a few weeks ago?"

"Oh, no. I don't think that was a real break-in. As you said then, the back door must have been blown open by the wind."

"Did your husband seem alarmed by the incident?"

"Well, to tell you the truth," Grace hedged, "I didn't exactly tell him about the false alarm."

"Not exactly?"

Grace shook her head. "I didn't want to upset him for nothing. He tends to worry."

Detective Hubbard laughed. "My wife probably wouldn't tell me either."

"Could we keep my little mistake of setting off a false alarm between us?" Grace pushed.

"You women love to keep your secrets, don't you," he teased.

Grace chaffed at his somewhat condescending tone, but resisted the urge to respond.

The door from the hallway swung open, and the real Mrs. Updike entered followed by a frantic Celina. Margaret opened the cabinet left of the sink and took out a bottle of Excedrin before filling a glass with spring water from the refrigerator. Detective Hubbard watched her for a moment, before resuming his conversation with Grace. "I created a list of the names and personal information guests provided and would like to cross check that with your list of the people who were invited. We'll need their names, addresses, telephone numbers and an explanation as to why they were invited, plus spouses and dates." He glanced at Romy. "Include caterers, musicians, household help, even the bartender."

Mrs. Updike turned to face him. "I'll have someone run it by your office tomorrow," she promised in a weary voice.

"And who are you?" Detective Hubbard questioned.

Margaret paused, the patrician of a woman accustomed to recognition rising to the top. "I am Margaret Updike, of course." She pushed the door to exit.

Detective Hubbard turned to Grace. "I thought you were Mrs. Updike."

"She is," Celina inserted before Grace could reply.

"That was the 'other' Mrs. Updike, her mother-in-law. She . . . helped a lot with the preparations, especially the invitation list."

The detective glanced back at the door through which Margaret had just exited. "She looks rather young to be the superintendent's mother."

"It's a wonder what they can do with facelifts these days," Romy declared.

The detective nodded, uninterested in participating in a discussion on facelifts. "Well, if you or your mother-in-law can get that list to us within a couple of days, we would certainly appreciate your assistance."

"Absolutely," Grace promised. She turned and wrote a note on the dry erase board hanging above the kitchen desk. "Send name and address of all attendees to Detective Hubbard."

He handed her his card. "You can e-mail me, if that's more convenient."

"Thank you. I'll do that."

Detective Hubbard returned to questioning guests in the family room, and Celina shadowed Margaret Updike to make sure the two did not meet again.

If the shooting occurred in slow motion, the end of the party fast-forwarded. Excused guests poured out of the mansion, anxious to remove themselves from danger, and more importantly, in search of yet another individual to whom they could tell their dramatic story.

Good breeding triumphed over trauma. Before leaving to join her husband at the hospital, a pale, but functioning Margaret Updike thanked everyone for coming and expressed assurance the superintendent would be perfectly fine.

Detectives Crooke and Hubbard worked on finishing up their report. They were almost done when Grace, not knowing they were in the family room, walked in for a last check of the place.

"Pardon us, Mrs. Updike," Sergeant Detective Crooke apologized, standing up. "I didn't realize you were still here. I thought someone said you left to join your husband at the hospital."

"That was the other Mrs. Updike," Detective Hubbard informed him.

"The other?" Detective Crooke repeated puzzled.

"Her mother-in-law," his partner nodded. Grace squirmed while Detective Hubbard took it upon himself to explain the situation to his partner. "Remember that tall woman who was standing near the superintendent when we first got here? She got pretty hysterical so they took her upstairs. You know the one . . . short hair, kind of poofed on top. She only looks about fifty, but the woman's had a facelift. Pretty good job too."

Thoroughly confused and somewhat embarrassed by his partner's soliloquy, Sergeant Detective Crooke looked at Hubbard as if he were a babbling idiot, which, no doubt, the sergeant thought he was at the moment. In an effort to get the man to stop talking, he focused the discussion back on Grace. "I'm sure this has been very difficult for you." He handed her his card. "If there's anything we can do to help or to make you feel more secure, please don't hesitate to call us."

"Thank you," Grace responded and retreated to the kitchen.

The evening was over. Ms. Cole took her place on the west side of the foyer, where she stood to the end, glowering as potential suspects passed her by. The Ladies of the Club, however, exited almost as fast as they had the night of their break-in.

Lara resided in a well-ordered, half-brick, half-cream siding tri-level. The neatly shoveled walk formed a ninety-degree angle, efficiently guiding guests from the driveway to the stoop, where a snow-swept door pad announced, "Hi, I'm Matt."

Her warm entryway opened to the sounds of domestic comfort. The living room's soothing earth tones set a welcoming pitch. The walnut wardrobe inherited from Max's family stood aligned against one wall, with an upright piano positioned tidily in a corner. A hardwood rocker and upholstered chair were pulled near the coffee table, intentionally positioned to encourage conversation. A gentle, lived-in feeling pervaded the regulated order providing the room with an overall sense of hominess and comfort.

Lara's efficient, eat-in kitchen overlooked the downstairs family room, where her husband and son argued good-naturedly over whose baseball team would take the pennant five months from now. Stairs led up to the bedrooms, where her daughter, Kelsey, labored over schoolbooks. The L-shaped living room's small leg revealed a walnut sideboard, china cabinet, and dining table. A simple brass chandelier hung from the room's center, highlighting the remains of the ladies' supper.

"There goes our primary suspect," Romy grumbled, curling her feet beneath her on the sofa. "He couldn't have shot himself. The doctor would have been able to tell that by the powder burns on his skin. It has to be someone else."

"Not necessarily. All the other evidence still points to him," Lara countered. "This instance might not be related to Winston or the theft."

Romy took a sip of her tea, carefully balancing her saucer on the arm of the sofa. "The gunman must have been shooting from some distance."

"Not to mention I would have known if a gun went off that close to my ear," Tamara added.

"Detective Crooke seemed pretty certain that it must have been fired through the window." Lara tapped her pencil on the blank tablet and wished she could think of something significant enough to note. Giving up, she began sketching the window of the Updike family room. She penciled in the members of the band, the dancers, and the guests in the room at the time of the shooting.

Celina sighed. "Do you realize how many people in between the window and the superintendent could have been accidentally shot?"

"Does that tell us the killer is a crack shot?" Tamara asked, rubbing her forehead.

"Or a crack pot?" Romy murmured.

"Maybe just desperate." Lara drew in the superintendent and Tamara.

"That's good," Grace commented, leaning over to see the sketch. "You really caught Tamara's expression." Grace studied the drawing a moment longer. "Tamara, take a look at this. Was this exactly the scene at the moment he was shot?"

Tamara moved to the sofa beside Lara to see the sketch. "That's close. We were talking so his head was bent forward a little more. The band was so loud that it was hard to hear. I complimented him on the wonderful party; he was giving all credit to his wife." Tamara sat back down in her chair before continuing. "He may not think his wife ever walked on water, but I bet he thinks she towed the disciples' boat out so Jesus would have somewhere to walk. Just before he was shot, I was thinking how incredible it must feel to be so loved by a man."

Lara re-sketched the superintendent, this time bowing his head and bending his shoulders slightly forward so his ear was close to Tamara's mouth. She paused, startled by the noticeable change in the bullet's flight path. "Tamara, take a look at this."

"Ugh, that bullet really did hit pretty close to me, didn't it? I'm glad your angle must be slightly off."

"What if it isn't?" she countered.

"It has to be. The bullet didn't hit me. I wouldn't have survived a gunshot fired at that angle."

"Perhaps this is the view the shooter saw half a second before pulling the trigger." Lara studied her drawing for a moment. "What if the bullet wasn't meant to shoot Updike? What if it was meant to kill you?"

"Me? Why on earth would anyone want to kill me? Other than my husband, that is."

"Why is anyone trying to kill all the other township employees?" Lara's crisp tone indicated her brain was rapidly processing the information and arriving at a deduction. "There are two reasons why most murders are committed—love and money. Nobody's killing off township employees over love. This is all about money."

"Why would the murderer go after me?"

"You know someone's stealing. You know they're doing it through ghost employees."

"But I don't know who is stealing!"

"The thief may think you do." Lara cautioned.

Celina focused on the crucial. "In that case, what are we going to do to protect Tamara? One missed shot won't stop a determined killer."

"The only way we can protect her is to discover the murderer's identity," Lara asserted. "Who had motive, means, and opportunity?"

Conversation stopped as each of the ladies weighed the question. Lara tapped her pencil against her pad, methodically reviewing the chain of events as she searched for a pattern. Celina narrowed her eyes, mentally scrutinizing each suspect's character. Grace considered character too, but wishing to believe the best in everyone, she searched for details that would exonerate each suspect. Tamara reached for a mint, her mind flitting between analyzing who had the best opportunity to steal the money and wondering if her kids were upset she was gone again tonight. Romy assessed the details of the St. Patrick's Day party, sifting each little particle of information in an attempt to differentiate between the noteworthy and the insignificant.

"Ms. Cole," Romy broke the peace.

"Why Ms. Cole?" Lara quizzed her. "What's her motive?"

"Jealousy. She's in love with Mr. Updike. I saw the way she glared when Tamara was dancing with the superintendent. Talk about hostile!"

"She wouldn't try to kill Tamara for that," Lara shook her head. "If jealousy were her motive, she would go after Mrs. Updike, not an underpaid accountant with four kids. No offence, Tamara," Lara apologized.

"None taken. I do have four kids, and I am underpaid."

"All of the evidence points to Ms. Cole," Romy insisted. "Sometimes the obvious is the answer."

"Sometimes," Lara agreed. "But if she's in love with Updike, why would she steal the money? It won't help her win him. When it comes out, Updike is the one who is going to look bad for letting it happen. I don't think she would want that to happen."

"She does come across as a one-woman protection unit," Romy sighed, reluctant to give up her theory.

Grace agreed. "I chatted with her for a few minutes after dinner. The objective of every word that came out of her mouth was to convince anyone who would listen that Superintendent Updike is the man of the hour, the week, and the year. She's the consummate spinmaster. The woman's so good she could work in Washington."

"If Updike ever ran for president, I bet she would," Celina predicted. "Speaking of the man of the hour, are we all set for our lunch with Greg tomorrow, Tamara?"

"Yes," Tamara acknowledged slowly. "I doubt if anything will make him change his mind. I appreciate that all of you want to help. Don't be too disappointed if he doesn't respond the way you want him to, okay?"

"We'll see," Celina smiled.

Greg Montgomery smiled at the hostess as he eased into the restaurant chair. This was turning out to be a pretty good day. Word was getting around the office that he was the top candidate for the new V.P. position. Two secretaries had offered to work on special projects if he needed them. Coworkers were already asking his opinion and treating him with the deference to which his new position would entitle him. Tamara wanted to have lunch together. She said she had a question to ask him. Greg smirked. Obviously, she wanted to come back home.

His gaze wandered to the waitress at the next table as he considered how his wife might phrase the request. She'd probably claim they should work things out for the sake of the children. For a moment, he considered telling her no. An empty house had been quite convenient for his social life. On the other hand, continually having to invent excuses for his wife's absence at business dinners was annoying. Oscar Coolidge, the CEO, was a grandfatherly type who believed in promoting stable young men. He defined stable as "happily married with children." According to Coolidge, a corporation of family men was "good for the company, good for the economy and good for America." Greg had heard the boss' speech so many times he could quote it verbatim. The subject irritated him. He glanced down at his watch with impatience, 11:30 exactly. Where was she, anyway?

"Hello, Greg. How are you?" a warm, female voice inquired.

Greg looked up to see three of his wife's closest friends, Celina, Romy, and Lara, making themselves comfortable at his table.

"Great, always great." Salesman's slick oozed out of him like an involuntary reflex. His gaze traveled from Celina in her chic Jones of New York business suit to Lara's steady unwavering gaze and then to Romy's piercing assessment. Greg shifted slightly in his chair to shake off a feeling of unease. Secure women always made him a bit nervous. "What are you three gorgeous women doing here?" he asked, trying to sound casual.

"We dropped by to see you," Celina shmoozed back. Business acquaintances who had met her across the negotiating table would have recognized the danger in her sweetness. "How's life treating you?"

Chapter Fourteen

"Not bad," Greg hedged, uncertain where the conversation was headed.

"I hear a promotion's in the works," she praised. "Congratulations."

Greg couldn't hold back a satisfied smile. If people at the company where Celina worked had heard about the promotion, it must be definite. "Well, you put in the long hours, beat the sales records, win the awards, and always hope it pays off."

Romy held back an inclination to gag and wished Celina would skip to the real purpose of their visit. Romy hated small talk with people she despised.

"It certainly looks like it's about to pay off big," Celina agreed. "In which case, it would be in your best interest to have the rest of your life in order so you can enjoy it."

Now they were getting somewhere. Tamara must have sent her friends as the advance team to butter him up so she could come home. "Yes, even with all the work accolades, my life still has an overlying sadness to it," he agreed. He was going to make them come right out and ask him to take her back. "It's hard to know what to do to make life right again. Do you have any suggestions?"

"As a matter of fact, we do. We would like you to drop the custody suit," Celina explained.

Greg put on his saddest look. "I never wanted a divorce. I was crushed when Tamara demanded it." His eyes filled with tears. "Our home, our dreams, the pain all of us, especially our children, have gone through. It will be difficult, but we need to try to make it work." He paused, unsure of his audience. Perhaps he should appear gracious. "It wasn't all Tamara's fault. I'm sure I wasn't the most attentive of husbands at times."

"Dating other women often makes one less attentive at home," Romy quipped.

Greg's face tightened with anger. Bored with the subject now that he was no longer cast in a favorable light, he snapped. "Where is Tamara anyway? If she wants me to take her back, she should come ask me herself and not send all of you to make me feel sorry for her."

Celina leaned forward to look him squarely in the eye. She spoke in quiet, measured tones. "You may have misunderstood us. We want you to drop the custody suit and move out of the house, so that Tamara and the kids can live there."

Stunned, Greg leaned back in his chair to increase his breathing space. "If I give her the house, where would I live?" he asked.

Romy gave him a genuine smile. "That would be your problem, wouldn't it? Perhaps you could find a nice singles condo for entertaining all your girlfriends." Greg's eyes flicked, but his expression failed to show signs of embarrassment.

"It's really the right thing to do, Greg," Celina continued. "The children need their home back. Surely, you want them to have it. I want to believe the best about you. I always liked you."

"I didn't," Romy spoke up.

"No, that's true. Romy never did like you. I, however, think you can be very funny on occasion. So for old times' sake, humor me now. Convince me you have your family's best interest at heart."

"Of course, I do," he protested. "If Tamara is intent on breaking up our home, then I guess I have no choice. I'll have my lawyer write something up."

Celina slid a document in front of him. "That won't be necessary. Romy already typed up the papers."

"I can't sign a paper without having my lawyer look it over. Someone needs to lookout for my best interest. What if it's not fair to me?"

"It's more than fair to you," Celina admitted. "By law, your wife is entitled to fifty percent of everything.

Under this agreement you keep the speed boat and the Lexus, even though it's new and her van is seven-years old. She's even declining a share in the lake cabin you inherited from your uncle."

"That's mine!" he snapped.

"Not according to Indiana law," Lara corrected. "But Tamara wanted your sisters to still use it. She said they have a lot of fun memories from their teen years."

"Letting you keep anything was against my advice," Romy clarified. "Personally, I think she should have taken you to the cleaners."

Greg picked up the document. He read the first two paragraphs, then stopped. "We currently have joint custody, with Tamara having primary residence. My lawyer has already filed a motion to reverse that so that I have primary custody and residence. Now you're asking me to give up decision-making power for my own children? You're crazy!"

Romy and Lara seethed inwardly, but kept silent. Celina smiled pleasantly. "Keep reading, Greg."

He resumed scanning the document, his eyes narrowing in selfishness. "I'm not paying for fifty percent of all this—a piano teacher, swimming lessons at the YMCA, a week of church camp. You expect me to give her fifty percent of our savings. Forget it." He pushed the papers back to Celina. He tilted his chin in confident arrogance as he leaned back in his chair. "It's not in my best interest for me to sign this."

"Actually, it is in your best interest," Celina encouraged him. "Look over there by the window. You see

Grace, don't you? She's standing beside your boss, Mr. Coolidge. He happens to be a good friend of the Pappas family. You see, if you don't sign, Grace is going to have an informative chat with Mr. Coolidge about how, in spite of that nice salary, your child support payments are six months in arrears. She will also tell him how you are shacking up with girlfriend after girlfriend in a 3,500 square foot house while your wife and five children are crowded into 900 feet of less than desirable living space. I wonder if Mr. Coolidge will want to promote such an irresponsible man to the position of vice-president?"

Greg stared at sweet, lovely, generous Grace absorbed in her conversation with the owner and CEO of Greg's company. As if on cue, Grace turned, beamed at him, and waved. Her friendliness encouraged him. "You're bluffing. Grace would never do that to me."

Celina sighed. "You still don't get it, Greg, do you? You're a little slower than I thought."

"I said he was," Romy reminded her.

"That's true, you did. Okay, Greg, pay attention. This is not about you. It's about Tamara and the kids. Grace would do *anything* for Tamara and the kids."

"Coolidge wouldn't believe her," he challenged, with more hope than conviction.

"He will when Tamara and the kids show up at the company picnic begging for grocery money."

"Tamara has too much pride to do that!"

"Possibly. But if that's uncomfortable for her, we can save her the embarrassment by showing him these."

This was the moment Romy had waited for. With more than a little flair, she tossed a manila packet across the table.

Greg shifted his shoulders back and opened the envelope in what he hoped was a nonchalant manner. Images of his children spilled out. The three girls sleeping in one bed; his son on a pallet in the living room; stacks of boxes still unpacked because there was no place to put them; too many people living in too little space. Then came half a dozen pictures of where he still lived: an elegant two-story brick house with detailed landscaping, formal dining and living rooms with wainscot and chair railing, custom woodwork throughout, a garden bath bigger than the room where his daughters slept.

Greg's bravado held up for a last stand. "She left me. I'll tell Coolidge she wants to live like that."

Romy burst into laughter, and threw another picture onto the table in front of him. This one revealed Greg and a pretty redhead, locked in a passionate embrace on the steps of the Montgomery family home.

"There's more," Celina promised softly.

Without another word, Greg pulled the agreement back toward him and signed it.

After church on Sunday, Tamara swung by the office. It wasn't that she needed to put in the extra time as much as she hated to go home to an empty house when the children were with Greg. Once seated at her desk, she tuned her radio to the best of the last three decades and relaxed.

This former officer's home with its architectural detail, front and back stairways, and gorgeous woodwork was a cozy place to work. From her desk, she could look out the front windows onto the deserted parade grounds covered with snow. By stretching, she could also see out the back to the alley where she had parked her car right next to the west door instead of hiking in from the employees' lot. That was another advantage to coming in on a Sunday afternoon.

Tamara flipped the switch to warm up her computer. Pulling several files out of her desk drawer, she focused her mind on work. In a little over ninety minutes, she completed the drama club expenses and the bi-annual cafeteria report. It always amazed her how much work she could get done without anyone else around.

Her mind migrated from quarterly outgo to wondering who was getting the extra paychecks. The answer had to be in the pattern of theft. A few clicks on her mouse and the computer screen revealed salary payouts by individual schools for the past twelve months. "The whole thing about the money going in and out of his account is so strange," she mused, as she walked to the microwave to heat a cup of water for tea.

Pulling a bag of mint chamomile from the cabinet, she let it steep while she continued her contemplation. "Evidently the superintendent is superstitious about withdrawing gambling money and that's why it has to end in seventy-seven, but he sure is meticulous with his thieving practices of nice round numbers.

For a brief moment, the possibility the Superintendent might have a split personality flitted across her mind. Dismissing the idea, she pulled the tea bag out and took a sip. Tea bags were a poor substitute for a satisfying cup of brewed tea, but at least it was hot. The office was chilly. The thermostat must automatically lower after five on weekends. She carried her mug back to her desk and sat down.

Oblivious to the empty office around her, Tamara flipped open a manila folder filled with printouts. As Cindy had so dramatically and so unoriginally proclaimed, one had to follow the money. Alright, that's what Tamara would do. The answer had to be here somewhere. She lifted her mug, eyes scanning the page. Without taking a sip, Tamara set the tea back down on the desk. That was it! That had to be what Cindy said that got her killed. She had quoted Winston as saying, 'Money always leaves a trail.' Could Updike have overheard her? Where were they when she said it? It happened after Tamara's encounter with Ms. Cole? Perhaps Ms. Cole repeated the conversation to the superintendent.

Money always leaves a trail. What was the trail? Who did it implicate? Reports proved only that someone was embezzling school funds. The reports didn't implicate a specific person. Updike had access to the money. He had a gambling problem. Close to the same amount he lost in gambling always reappeared in his bank account. How much circumstantial evidence did the law require to convict a man of robbery?

Until he was shot, the superintendent appeared guilty. But if one accepted the premise that Updike was indeed the thief, then the thief and the murderer had to be two different people. He couldn't have shot himself. Did he have a partner? Had a disagreement turned the partnership deadly? Who was most likely to be his partner?

Opportunity pointed to Ms. Cole. She had access to the financial books and computers. If she couldn't get the man, was she going for the money? Her bank account indicated the possibility. Perhaps the money in her account wasn't really from Wal-Mart stock.

Snippets of conversations from the past several weeks swirled round Tamara's mind. Somehow it all connected: the superintendent's gambling, the deposits almost equaling the withdrawals. Or did she have that backward? Did the deposit slips equal the withdrawals or did the withdrawals equal the deposit slips? Was the stolen money gambled or was the gambled money replaced?

Updike was definitely withdrawing money from his account and gambling it away. They knew that to be fact. Could someone else be replacing the funds for him? Feeling like she was on to something, Tamara continued her train of thought. The theft was very well done, almost untraceable. The murders were impeccable, flawless, and fastidious in their perfection. That wasn't characteristic of the superintendent. He could more accurately be described as laid-back. The school board had hired Richard Updike for his excellent social skills. He was good at his job because people enjoyed working for him. He had an instinct for when to demand more and when to be lenient. He pushed township staff for excellence, but not for perfection.

The murderer, on the other hand, had to be someone who didn't miss a detail. That adjective better described her soon-to-be ex-husband. Greg was rotten on the inside, but if he were going to commit a murder, he would do it well. They were dealing with an excellent murderer.

Ms. Cole was excellent at her job, but she didn't fit the role of an excellent murderer. The theft had a natural finesse never apparent in the administrative assistant's labor. The way ghost employees floated from school to school, never staying on the books of any one building for more than a month, did not evidence cleverness typical of Ms. Cole. Ms. Cole did not glide through life, she plodded. Her skill lay in having become so proficient at her work that she plodded fast enough to be regarded an expert. But this thief had polish.

Tamara pictured Updike's bank slip lying on the carpet. Something was missing. Like the con man's coconut game at the fair, money appeared, disappeared, and then reappeared. The pattern floated loosely in her mind. Then nothing—it was gone. Tamara shook her head in frustration. She almost had it. Walking back to the sink, she rinsed out her cup and returned to her desk.

Start over at the beginning, she instructed herself.

Everything connected to Updike. If it wasn't him, perhaps someone wanted to make him look bad? Images of people surrounding the superintendent whirled through her mind. She visualized each face, scrutinizing the character and temperament, dissecting personal agendas. One by one she imagined possible motives until her list of suspects ran out. No one, not one person had a motive for making him look bad. People genuinely liked the man. They all wanted him to look good.

So then, did the question become who wanted him to look good the most? Startled by the possibility, Tamara tapped her pencil against her desk, reconsidering the suspects as overzealous advocates for the superintendent. She was looking for someone inventive, resourceful, an artful tactician, clever to the point of cunningness. She stopped tapping as the solution clicked into place. Understanding flooded her mind. Tamara knew the murderer's identity and motive.

Everything made sense, including the withdrawal statement. Her solution hinged on the question she had asked herself earlier. Was the stolen money gambled or was the gambled money replaced? Was the money replaced by someone who wanted the superintendent's life to be beyond smooth, even perfect? Motive glared so clearly she felt stupid for not having seen it sooner. This theft was about perfection. The murders, the perfect murders, were simply a method of erasing a smudge in the illusion.

The only thing she couldn't figure out was how the murderer accessed the books. Distracted by the unraveling of the mystery, Tamara failed to hear the sound of a door opening and closing. She hit the speaker button and punched Romy's number.

"Kelly residence."

"Romy, it's me."

"Hey me. What are you doing?"

"I'm working."

"On a Sunday? You need to get out more often, Tamara. You can't work all the time." Oblivious to the urgency in Tamara's voice, Romy chatted on. "We should go shopping next week or out for lunch. We could go to Yen Ching's. They have the best tasting and most authentic Chinese food in Indianapolis."

"Romy, listen." Tamara's words came out in a rush. "I need to know which came first. Think about the deposits and withdrawals of Updike's bank account. Did the amount withdrawn match the number already deposited or did it match the deposit that came after it?"

"First the money was withdrawn, and then it was redeposited. Why do you ask?"

"I know who killed Winston and Cindy. It was Margaret Updike."

"Mrs. Updike? Why on earth do you think it's her?"

"The money disappears from the township, but consistently reappears in his bank account," Tamara explained. "He gambles their family money away. She steals the township money, and then puts in just enough to cover his losses. If the superintendent was the one stealing, he would just lose whatever he took out. That's not happening. She's replacing what he loses."

Romy's voice on the other end sounded doubtful. "So why did she try to kill her husband?"

"She didn't. Lara was right. Margaret was trying to shoot me. Either she thought Cindy told me too much or she thought I figured it out."

"But she could have accidentally killed the superintendent. Why would she take that kind of chance?"

"It never occurred to her she'd miss. She's beyond confident. She's haughty to the point of arrogance, Machiavellian. People don't think of her as arrogant because she hides her egotism behind a layer of sophistication and good manners."

Romy tried again. "If the superintendent didn't know, why did he cover up for her by claiming Winston called in sick when he was already dead?"

"The superintendent never said he spoke with Winston himself. He said Winston called in sick. His wife probably gave him that message because she needed time to get rid of the body."

Tamara could hear Romy turning the faucet on. That meant she was deep in thought scrubbing the table as she thought through the possibility. Sounds of scrubbing finally ceased, and Romy objected, "Mrs. Updike doesn't have the right personality for a murderer."

"Of course, she does. Margaret Updike's personality is exactly the type of murderer who never gets caught. Think about it. She stole and murdered beautifully, just as she does everything else. The police can't prove the two deaths are connected. The theft hasn't even been discovered by anybody official yet."

Romy spoke slowly, in direct contrast to Tamara's torrent of words. "But why would she murder Winston? And why would she steal? Her husband has the gambling addiction. The money hides his sins, not hers."

"Exactly. Money wasn't the motive. It was obsession. She's the perfect wife, the woman every man dreams of having. In addition to being beautiful, her whole life revolves around making sure his world runs smoothly. She did it *for* her husband—to cover up his gambling so no one would find out. He gambles the money away. She covers his tracks by putting it back. The family maintains an unaffected existence."

"Wouldn't he notice they're never low on cash, even though he's gambling it away?" Romy questioned.

"He might assume she noticed the account was low and simply cashed in a CD or took money from her inheritance. Another thing to keep in mind is that addicts, whether they are addicted to drugs, alcohol or gambling, don't look too hard to discover where the extra money is coming from. They're just glad it keeps coming, and their habit isn't being interrupted. The last thing they want is a confrontation that could make continuing their habit more difficult."

"Do you have any physical proof at all?"

"None. I searched his office the night of the party. His files contained only withdrawal slips. I thought something was wrong at the time, but I couldn't figure out what it was. Then Mrs. Updike came into the room to get a book, and I had to hide in the closet until she was gone. One of the withdrawal slips was on the floor.

I thought sure she was going to see it and catch me. Think about it. The woman keeps everything in her house in perfect order. Why would she separate the bank slips? Even if she didn't know why he was making the withdrawals, she would have to know he's taking money out. Naturally, she would want to keep all of the banking information together. It doesn't make sense for such a methodical woman to be unorganized in only one area of her life. She had to have a purpose for deviating from the norm."

"People don't generally deviate from their routine without a pretty powerful motive," Romy agreed. "So, then, the motive for murder was cover up and the motive for the theft was . . . love?"

"Not love. We can't call it that. I would say the motive was money to continue the illusion of a perfect life. The superintendent must have told her Winston was reviewing the books to see if money was missing. Winston may have shown up at their home early in the evening asking to talk to Updike. She must have lured him to the basement on the pretext of seeing the superintendent and then killed Winston with an ice pick. The only thing I can't figure out is how Mrs. Updike accessed the township account."

"That's simple enough. If you can access the Internet, you can find a site that will teach you how to do anything you want to do, all within the privacy of your own home."

Tamara tapped her pencil against her mug. "So how do we prove she's the one stealing funds?"

Romy considered the technical possibilities. "If she accessed the administration computers from home, her hard drive will have a record of it."

"Wouldn't she have erased those files?"

"Probably but the computer will still have a record of it. Most people assume they're deleting a file from the hard drive when they empty the recycle bin. All they're really doing is getting rid of the pointer that tells them where the file is located on the hard drive. The file itself is still there. The right software can bring it back."

Tamara shook her head in disbelief of her own theory. "She seems so perfectly normal. The woman must have some type of personality disorder."

A hand reached out from behind Tamara. *Click.* The line went dead as a flawlessly manicured index finger held the switch hook down. Tamara's eyes followed the arm up the shoulder to confront the speculative face of Margaret Updike.

"Mrs. Updike, I didn't hear you come in." Tamara floundered for some polite phrase, desperately wondering what the woman had overheard and how it could be explained away. "How long have you been here?"

"Don't treat me as stupid, dear. It's bad manners."

"No, of course not. I . . . was just talking with a friend."

Margaret pulled a .22 caliber semi-automatic handgun out of her purse. "So I heard. I found your conversation fascinating. So much so that it was difficult to keep quiet, especially when you struggled over how I accessed the files. I wanted to help you with the details, but first I needed to hear how much you and your friend know. You were on target except, of course, for the part about the personality disorder." Margaret smiled. "Surely you realize I am much too organized to have a personality disorder."

She chuckled at her own joke before continuing. "What name did you call your friend? Romy? Unusual name, easy to remember." Recognition dawned and Margaret's expression changed. "Romy," she repeated. "Surely not . . ." The fear in Tamara's face confirmed it. Throwing back her head, Margaret gave a deep laugh. "The caterer! My, my, I did underestimate you. Well, that won't happen again. Too bad to lose such a good caterer. I was thinking about using them again next year. Perhaps Bon Appetit can replace her. Too bad," she repeated. "Very polite girl. So nice the way she identifies herself when answering the phone—Kelly Residence. That will be very helpful when I need to find her."

"Why do you need to find her?" Tamara fought to keep her voice calm.

"So I can kill her. I can't have that telephone call be your last known conversation. She would tie me to your murder. No one would believe that, of course. I'm far too respectable to attract serious suspicion. However, I do hate to have my name connected with even a hint of gossip. I promised Richard long ago that I would be like Caesar's wife—above reproach at all times."

The ring of the telephone interrupted their exchange. Both women glanced down at the caller I.D.

"Romy called back," Margaret observed with a smile. "Evidently she thinks you were accidentally disconnected." Tamara reached for the receiver as she tried to think of some normal sounding sentence that would alert Romy to the danger.

"Don't answer that," Margaret commanded.

Tamara hesitated as the phone rang. Margaret cocked her gun, pointed it directly at Tamara's head, and smiled. "I couldn't possibly miss at this range; even if I am . . . I believe the word you used was *arrogant.*"

Chapter Fifteen

Tamara locked eyes with Margaret Updike. The phone rang sixteen times before stopping. Both women silently counted.

By the third attempt, it took Romy three seconds to dial. This time it died in the middle of the eighth ring. The silence didn't bring the anticipated peace, but merely an empty stillness. The phone did not ring again.

Tamara groped for a question that would break the stillness and induce her opponent to talk. "How did you know that I would be here today?"

"I didn't, actually. That was just good luck. I dropped by to make a few minor adjustments in the salary schedule. Generally, I do that from my home computer during the week, but since Richard has taken a few days off to recover from the accident, I needed a bit more privacy."

"The accident," what a strange way to refer to having shot one's husband. Tamara continued to play for time, all the while knowing that, even if Romy suspected something was wrong, it was not physically possible for her to drive out to the fort in time to be of help. "He doesn't know about the extra teachers on the payroll?" she asked.

"Of course not. He would never have agreed to the little bonuses I arranged. He deserves the extra money, but is far too humble to take it. Besides, I would never bother my husband with the particulars of a plan. You were absolutely right when you told your friend my focus is on making sure Richard's life runs smoothly. He doesn't need to know the details of how I make it happen, only that I am the one who makes his world function." She smiled, pleased with herself. "It is quite satisfying to have a grateful husband. Come on, time to get up."

She's using the same tone she would to get her children out of bed in the morning. Tamara struggled for another diversionary question. "Did Winston or Ms. Cole know you were the ghost employee?"

Margaret shook her head. "Winston suspected Richard. Imagine his thinking Richard would take school funds for himself! Winston deserved to die for being so stupid. He realized the salary adjustments were being made from our home computer. What a nuisance! He almost made us late for *The Lion King* because it took so long to shove him in the closet." She paused to consider the incident. "He died quickly, though, and that was nice. I hit him in exactly the right spot. Fortunately, I took Anatomy in college and remembered just where to shove the ice pick."

Tamara marveled at the woman's ability to mix psychotic thinking with a polite tone and have it come out sounding almost like a rational chat.

Margaret continued. "Amy knew about the early-morning meeting between the superintendent and Winston. She searched the records until she was able to produce a spreadsheet highlighting your financial inconsistencies. Amy didn't think you were stealing; she simply hoped to have you fired for incompetence. By the way, I helped you out there. I encouraged Richard to give you more time to get your life back together."

"You're not . . . you're not going after Ms. Cole, too, are you?" Tamara asked the question tentatively, half afraid of planting the idea in her murderous head.

"Of course not." Margaret looked at Tamara as if she thought her half daft. "Amy is far too valuable to dispose of. She does a marvelous job keeping things orderly here at the office."

Tamara swallowed hard before continuing with her questions. "Why were the problems only on the accounts where I worked?"

"I made all the changes on your work so that if a discrepancy were discovered, Richard and Winston would assume you were the problem."

"But why me?"

"You were the most believable. Everyone would assume your mind was on your divorce and children instead of your work. I knew Richard would feel sorry for you, as he did, and not look so deeply into your accounting errors that it would be uncomfortable for me. He didn't even want you to realize how many mistakes you had made because he was afraid you would feel bad. He told Winston to correct the problems and let you think you simply misunderstood the numbers."

"Was it necessary to kill Cindy?" Tamara asked, her tone wistful.

"That girl was a ditz. Every thought she ever had came right out of her mouth. However, that was convenient when I needed to know how to kill her. I didn't want to stab her because I preferred the police not think of her death as related to Winston's unfortunate demise. A suicide was much more convenient."

"Cindy didn't tell me what Winston told her. He may not have told her anything. Cindy . . . enjoyed talking."

Margaret nodded. "I chatted with her in the parking lot on Friday, hoping she would tell me what she knew, but she wouldn't. The silly thing kept insisting I come for tea. She had her heart set on a visit, babbling about what a wonderful time we would have, as if we were two confidantes gathering for gossip. So I came, and I brought the tea." Margaret smiled, as if pleased with herself for having the good manners to bring a hostess gift. "Winston hadn't really told her anything, but by then it was too late. She was such a foolish girl, not at all discreet. A visit from her boss's wife would have been the social event of her year. She would have told everyone about our little tête-à-tête. Detective Crooke would have been suspicious and wanted to know why I was there. What plausible reason could I have given for stopping by the girl's apartment? Even my husband might have asked questions. That would not have been good."

Margaret's tea party tone gave the discussion a *Through the Looking Glass* feel. The woman was talking about plausible reason as if an act of murder could in any way be a prudent option. Tamara directed the conversation to something concrete. "How long did it take you to break into the township's computer system?"

"I didn't break in." Margaret's tone was indignant. "I used Richard's access code. At first, I took money from our savings to cover the losses due to Richard's illness. It is an illness, you know. I studied up on it as soon as I realized his problem. Unfortunately, our own funds would have eventually run out, so I had to come up with a second plan. When Richard suffered a bad bout of pneumonia, he was off work for two weeks. Winston programmed the home and office computers with software that allowed Richard to access and review financial files from home. The computer access provided a perfect solution."

Margaret's voice acquired a rich tenor, as she indulged herself in a rare review of past triumphs. "It was kind of you to say that I am the wife every man dreams of having. I would simply say I used a bit of ingenuity to solve my husband's problem, creative project management one might call it."

Tamara struggled for a non-antagonizing response in the face of the woman's narcissism. The woman truly believed the world revolved around the Updike family. She viewed all other people as insignificant, dispensable extras in her family's personal play.

Margaret continued with her observations. "Most of what you said about me was very complimentary, although I never considered myself a Machiavellian type personality. I'll have to give that some thought. Niccolò Machiavelli was very misunderstood. I quite admire him."

Tamara put her hand casually on the desk and inched it towards the scissors.

"Just for the record," Margaret corrected, "I did see the withdrawal slip on the floor, but I didn't know who had been there until a few minutes later when I saw you walk out of the office." The woman was unwilling to be caught lacking even in her dishonesty. "Enough chit-chat. I have to be home by five so the superintendent can have dinner by six. Fortunately, I thought ahead and put a roast and vegetables in the crock pot. Take your coat with you, dear. We can't leave it here."

Tamara stood, and her eyes again lit on the scissors. If she could reach them, she would at least have a weapon if they got into a scuffle. Gathering her coat as directed, she tried to grab the scissors in the same sweeping motion. Margaret snatched the scissors. "I don't think so, dear. You don't need them and since I don't have the element of surprise, stabbing won't work with you. Let's put them back where they belong." Margaret tucked them tidily away in Tamara's desk. "Put your coat on now."

"Where are we going?" Tamara questioned, trying another stalling tactic as she slid her arms into her coat.

This time the delay provoked her captor's anger. Margaret's face scrunched into a momentary scowl, but a lifetime of proper responses forced her to immediately compose her face back into a socially acceptable expression. Seeming to relent of her harsh reaction, she explained, "I can't kill you in the office. That might reflect back on Richard. Finding your dead body on the trail where Winston was killed will support the theory that there's a lunatic with a fetish for people out for a winter's stroll. Pity I couldn't get Cindy out on the trail. It would have been so much simpler."

Tamara paused to push Cindy's office chair back into place as a means of hindering their process. "Perhaps you should have tried to get me out on the jogging trail earlier," she challenged. "You could have avoided shooting your husband."

Pain slapped Margaret across the face so visibly Tamara almost felt ashamed for having caused it. "That was horrible!" the superintendent's wife confided, "the worst moment of my life. I could not believe I had caused the man I love such pain." She redirected her anger toward Tamara. "That was your fault! If you hadn't been snooping around, I wouldn't have had to use the gun. I will stop you from ever harming Richard again." Margaret's patrician features curdled, for a moment and then, with the speed of a television edit, appeared pleasant again.

Tamara edged away from the woman in an effort to put the desk between them.

"That won't help," Margaret commented dryly. "I can shoot you from either side of the desk."

"You realize that if you shoot me, the police will be able to trace the bullet back to you. They have your gun on file now."

"Don't be silly. This is a new gun."

"All guns are registered," Tamara insisted, hoping the gun hadn't been bought illegally.

"You ought to be more informed, dear. Have you never heard of the gun show loophole? One doesn't have to be approved to buy guns at a trade show."

Tamara appealed to the woman's vanity. "But you're an unusually beautiful woman. The police will ask at trade shows. The dealers will remember you."

"Even if my disguise didn't work, I doubt if the dealers will be anxious to identify a customer. Why would they want to help the police solve a crime committed with a weapon they sold? That would be bad for future business. Now get moving before I decide shooting you here and now is worth the risk."

As Tamara turned to face the door, an obnoxious siren screamed and the fire sprinkler sprayed the room. A jet stream of cold water flattened Tamara's bangs, blocking her vision.

Six and a quarter miles of winding roads away, Romy sat back from her computer and waited. It had taken several minutes for her modem to access the computer system connected to the township's fire sprinkler system and another long minute to set it off. She prayed that whatever had happened, the diversion had been a help to Tamara

Tamara wheeled around to search out the alarm's source. No sight of flames. Had the alarm detected smoke or was there someone else in the building? Ignoring the siren's wail, she shoved hair out of her eyes and ducked behind Cindy's desk. She shivered as a spray of water from the cold sprinkler system trickled down her back. Taking a deep breath, Tamara attempted to smell the fire's location by inhaling. Nothing. How could she get safely out of the building without being trapped by flames or shot by Margaret when she couldn't even tell where the fire was burning? She could see the toes on Margaret's Italian leather flats less than three feet away. Tamara scooted backwards, putting a second desk between them, and then a third. If she could avoid getting shot or burnt to a crisp during the next five minutes that would give the fire department enough time to arrive and rescue her.

Margaret turned around to find her prey missing. "You might as well come out where I can see you! You are only delaying the inevitable and wasting my time."

Unwilling to reveal her hiding place, Tamara said nothing. The silence agitated Margaret. "I took care of that empty-headed twit, Cindy, and genius boy, Winston. A little housewife who couldn't hold on to her husband certainly isn't any competition."

Tamara flinched, but chose to ignore the taunting. She assessed her options as the sprinkler system continued to drench the office. She couldn't make a run for the front door without moving into Margaret's gun sight. The basement was an old coal cellar without a door to the outside. Tamara would be trapped without a window possibility of escape.

"You are trying my patience," the voice of one not used to having her patience tried rose in irritation.

Tamara studied the main hallway as a potential refuge. With a little luck, she might reach it, but if she stayed where she was, it was only a matter of time before Margaret found her. Then, she would be cornered with nowhere to go. The heavy walnut stairwell stood on the other side of the hallway. Tamara scrutinized Margaret's position in the room, trying to determine what her assailant could see. The thick banister and two thirds of the staircase were definitely visible, but Margaret might not be able to see the far side of the steps. If Tamara could crawl to the stairwell and remain out of sight until she reached the second floor, she could cross the corridor, sneak down the back stairs and escape out the west door before Margaret realized she had disappeared.

"Quit wasting my time." The pitch of Margaret's voice escalated with each sentence until it reached shrieking. "I'll get you."

Tamara shivered as her brain made a weird connection between Margaret's voice and the Wicked Witch of the West screeching, "I'll get you, my pretty, and your little dog too." The woman was unhinged. Fear eliminated Tamara's indecision. She would attempt to reach the second floor and escape down the back stairs.

Tamara inched her way behind Roger's desk. Her heart pounded a warning to not move. "Don't think about her," she admonished herself. "Focus on where you're going, not on where she's looking. You can't do anything about her, but you can move yourself to safety."

Keeping low to the floor, Tamara scooted around the doorframe and into the hall. She removed both her shoes at the bottom of the stairs to prevent them from clunking against the wood. Shoes in hand, she progressed upward in measured, steady fashion, crowding close by the papered wall on her left. She placed a light hand on each step, listening for creaking before hoisting a knee to that spot, and then repeated the process on subsequent steps. After only three stairs, her knees ached with resentment at the tortuous, unyielding hardwood, but she kept moving.

The fifth step squeaked from the pressure of her knee. Not much noise, but even the sound of her own clothes rustling as she moved fueled the pounding of her heart. Unwilling to retreat, she advanced, each step shrouded in more darkness and safety than the one before. On the seventh step, she paused to let out her breath. Fire engines wailed, still too distant to provide hope of rescue.

The patter of water fell on desks, books and floor providing an unchanging background to Tamara's own movements. Tamara cocked her head, trying to analyze the overall stillness. Something was wrong. There was an absence of a disturbance she ought to hear. Tamara closed her eyes and focused on identifying the lost sound. She opened her eyes and knew what was missing. Margaret had stopped calling. None of the noises could be attributed to the superintendent's wife. Tamara shot a glance to the bottom of the stairs to see if the woman was there—no one. Perhaps she had fled the building to escape the fire engines wailing dangerously close now. It took all of Tamara's self-control to resist leaning sideways over the banister to peep into the accounting room and locate her nemesis.

Head down to avoid hitting the thick banister, Tamara willed herself to continue crawling upwards, hand moving first, followed by knee, straining to hear any noise that would enlighten her to Margaret's presence.

A few more steps up and her fingers tapped the open space of hardwood floors. She could see nothing in the darkness of the landing, but welcomed the promise of concealment. Still shaking from the physical exertion of crawling inch by inch, Tamara stood gratefully and stumbled forward, her only goal to reach the back stairs and disappear out the door.

As she neared the center of the landing, Margaret sauntered out of the shadows. She had anticipated Tamara's plan of escape and snuck up the back stairs.

"You're making this much more difficult than it needs to be," the superintendent's wife disapproved.

Anger inundated Tamara's spirit, drowning what was left of fear and finishing this competition of wits. Tamara hurled Margaret back against the flight of stairs leading up to the third floor. Without pausing to see where her assailant had landed, Tamara ran toward the back stairs. In the semi-darkness, she knocked her hip into the walnut post. Ignoring the pain, she raced down the steps.

Behind her, she could hear Margaret scrambling to her feet. Margaret reached the stairs and paused to shoot. The first shot touched the ground floor landing a good six inches from Tamara's feet. Tamara rounded the stair post and pushed open the heavy wooden door leading to the building's back foyer. A second shot flew past her head before embedding itself in the paneling. Margaret's steps rapped on the floor signaling she was gaining on her prey. Tamara yanked the back door open as a third bullet split the frame. She launched herself down the porch steps, barely maintaining an upright position. Ignoring the possibility of help as fire engines screamed their arrival on Lawton Loop, Tamara raced to her van, pawing through her coat pocket for keys, and then jerking the door open and hiking herself into the driver's seat. Her old van threw snow to all sides, leaving a trail of burned oil as she gunned the motor and sped off down the back alley.

The fire engine and ambulance raced to a stop on the

other side of the administration building. Margaret Updike positioned herself in line with the outside door, fir-
ing the last of her wild shots into the alley as the fire
chief called for police backup.

Chapter Sixteen

Shortly after eleven that evening, the five club members each made a trip to the local grocery store. Shrouded in the parking lot's darkest corner, they crowded close to plan their strategy. Lara led the discussion. "We need a system for protecting Tamara and Romy. Margaret made it clear she intends to kill them both. Tamara's escape will make her more desperate, not less."

"Why didn't the police arrest Margaret for shooting up the administrative office?" Romy asked.

Hugging herself to stop the shivering, Grace replied. "I talked to my mother, who knows the fire chief's wife. The story is Mrs. Updike stopped by the office to pick up some papers for the superintendent to work on at home. A drifter trying to get in from the cold surprised her, and she overreacted, which was, of course, very natural considering her husband is still recovering from being shot by an intruder."

"A drifter?" Tamara protested, "At the administration building? Who's going to believe that?"

"It's not a question of who will believe it; it's a statement that no one is going to question. Her husband is the superintendent of schools. Whatever she says is going to be accepted at face value."

"So how are we going to keep Tamara and Romy safe?" Lara directed the conversation back to the immediate problem.

Grace glanced over at Tamara's van, where the four Montgomery children were sleeping. "Tamara has agreed she and the children will stay at my home until this is settled."

Celina brushed back a strand of hair the wind kept blowing in her eyes. "What about you, Romy? Margaret knows your name. I'm sure by now she knows your address as well."

"Don't worry about me. My house is safe." Romy added, "We have double-bolts and a security system that would even take me a while to bypass."

Lara hesitated, and then nodded. She knew Romy couldn't be talked into anything she didn't want to do. "That takes care of the nights, but you both have to go to work and take care of your families during the day. The problem is we don't know who Margaret is going after first, so we don't know where to focus our protection." Lara thought for a moment, and then suggested, "Instead of dividing our resources to protect the two of you, we'll watch her. I have tomorrow off. I can shadow Margaret while you're working. Grace, if necessary, can you follow her on Wednesday?"

"Absolutely."

"Good. That way we'll know what Margaret is up to, and it will also provide enough time for us to help Margaret incriminate herself."

"We need to get back inside the mansion and retrieve those deleted files so they'll show up on her hard drive," Romy asserted.

"And then we have to induce the police to check out the hard drive on Margaret's home computer," Celina added.

"Can you retrieve the deleted files?" Grace questioned.

Romy stomped her feet to ward off the freezing cold. "Yes, I bought recovery software last fall after Ian played around on my computer and deleted an appraisal it took me three days to complete. Give me fifteen minutes with her computer, and ninety-five percent of those deleted files will be right back where we want them."

"Is it ethical to retrieve files on someone else's computer?" Grace probed, not sure she wanted to hear the answer.

"The FBI does it all the time," Romy asserted in a firm voice.

Grace decided not to push an issue she clearly would not win. "In that case, let's get it done. This time," she added, wrapping her woolen scarf tighter around her neck and head, "you do what you want, but I'm going in through the front door." She sketched out her idea for being welcomed back to the Updike mansion.

"That's good," Lara agreed. "Now here's what I have in mind for helping Margaret incriminate herself." The ladies huddled close together, planning their counter attack, while blustery weather smacked their faces and subzero winds burned their ears. Warmed by their passion, they finalized plans to protect their own and bring Margaret to justice.

Monday found Tamara, Romy, Celina, and Grace back in the routine of their day-to-day lives packing lunches, driving carpools, and starting a new work week. Lara sent the kids in early with her school teacher husband, and was parked down the street from the Updike mansion when the school bus picked up the superintendent's children. The bus had barely disappeared around the corner towards the elementary school, when Margaret's Capri blue Mercedes exited the mansion's long driveway. "Looks like we've got a busy day ahead," Lara murmured to herself.

The luxury sedan shot down 113th Street turning south on Olio Road, barely hesitating at cross roads until backed up traffic forced a stop by Pendleton Pike. Turning right on to the state road, she wove in and out of traffic, annoying other drivers and making it easy for Lara to follow without being seen. Immediately before Franklin Road, Margaret whipped her car into a business lot on the north side of the street. She parked behind the Dumpster and hurried into the store.

Lara passed the building, turning right on to Franklin and then backtracking through parking spaces to obtain a discreet view of Margaret's movements.

The brick building had been painted a clean white twenty years earlier, but ignored ever since. Glazed windows and a darkly tinted door protected the privacy of all clientele. Lara read the small cardboard placard announcing PELFREY PAWNSHOP. "What on earth could she be pawning?" Lara muttered.

Hardly were the words out of her mouth before Margaret exited accompanied by a slightly built young man sporting half a dozen tattoos and a sad attempt at a goatee. Margaret moved quickly and, pressing a button on her key ring, popped the trunk. He lifted out a Gateway computer with an eighteen-inch screen.

"She's pawning her own computer to get rid of the evidence." Lara reclined against her seat in amazement, watching as the two walked back into the building. "How will we get the police to connect the deleted files to her now?" Picking up her cell phone, she punched in seven numbers and hit enter. "Grace, there's been a change of plans." Their conversation continued for several minutes before being cut short by Margaret's exit from the parking lot.

Lara waited five minutes before walking into the pawnshop. Tinkling bells announced her entry. The same young man who had assisted Margaret stood smiling behind the register. "I want to buy a computer," Lara informed him. "That Gateway there on the counter looks perfect."

Chapter Seventeen

The old officer's mansion had withstood many misfortunes in its almost one hundred years. Drenched offices awaited administration staff on Monday morning. Instead of their usual reports, several days would be spent cleaning up the aftermath of an effective sprinkler system. Cleaning crews mopped up standing puddles. Computers remained off until technical staff could assess the damage. Individual papers left out over the weekend were now plastered against the desk and in need of scraping up. Employees discovered even automated rain storms have a silver lining. Ms. Cole's cumbersome procedural manual, surreptitiously labeled *1001 Steps to Completing the Unnecessary,* was accidentally dropped in a waste basket steeped with water. It was a total loss.

Tamara was in the process of wiping down her desk

when she spotted Margaret Updike entering the administration offices. Impeccably dressed as always, the perfect wife balanced two large bakery boxes in her arms. Stricken, Tamara hovered behind a not-quite-tall-enough file cabinet to listen. Surely, the woman wouldn't try to kill her right here in front of everyone.

"Mrs. Updike, how nice to see you," the receptionist greeted her. "May I help you with those boxes?"

"Thank you, Sylvia. I thought I'd bring pastries from the Heidelberg Cafe for everyone to celebrate the superintendent's first day back at work. Where would you like them?"

"How kind of you! Why don't we set them in the break room? Mmm, delicious." Sylvia led the boss's wife to the converted kitchen, where they placed the selection of pastries on the countertop. Ms. Cole appeared and instructed Sylvia to pull out paper plates, napkins, and serving utensils.

Tamara played at working, her mind a jumble of questions and fear as she dried and redried the same desk accessories. Smiling, Mrs. Updike loaded a plate with three of the most sumptuous-looking pastries, poured a cup of coffee, and stopped beside Tamara's desk. Tamara looked up and saw the evil queen offering her bright red apples in the form of strudel. "I noticed you were so busy you didn't get anything to eat, so I brought you something."

"Thank you. Unfortunately, I started a new diet last week."

"Oh, but you simply must try these. They're from the

Heidelberg Café. I would be insulted if you didn't have at least a bite," Margaret insisted.

"Thank you," Tamara repeated, and taking the plate, she sat it down on her desk.

"It's such a beautiful day, isn't it?" Margaret continued.

Tamara's gaze turned to the windows, where the cold March wind shivered through the trees and smacked the faces of anyone foolish enough to venture outside.

"Perhaps not weather-wise," Margaret conceded, "but it's certainly a productive day, for me, anyhow. I've thrown out my old computer and am on my way to buy a new one, something fresh with no memory and full of empty files."

She's telling me I can't prove a thing, Tamara thought to herself. She bit her lip and tried to think of a nonantagonizing comment. The goal was for her to help Margaret view her and Romy as less of a threat until the club could gather conclusive evidence. "That sounds like a victory for you. Everyone needs a clean, fresh start once in a while."

Margaret beamed. "My thoughts exactly. Now if you'll excuse me, I'll go fix a plate for my husband. You know how I strive to be the perfect wife."

Grace took a deep breath, pushed the doorbell and listened to the chimes announcing her arrival at the Updike mansion. She'd never tell the others, but getting access to the computers while Margaret was home really wasn't less frightening. "Although it is more legal," she comforted herself as Margaret swung the door open.

"Grace, dear, what a surprise! Come in, come in. Can you believe how long this winter is lasting?"

"I am so sorry to drop by unannounced," Grace apologized.

"It's always a pleasure to see you, dear. Here, let me take your coat. I was just about to brew tea. Won't you have a cup with me?"

"Sounds perfect," Grace smiled.

"One moment then." Margaret, the perfect hostess and murderer, disappeared down the hallway.

Grace perched on the edge of the living room sofa, and then forced herself to sit back. It was crucial to their plan that she she appear natural. Up to this point, Margaret had never doubted Grace's motives or associated her with the theft in any way. If Margaret became suspicious now, it could endanger her life, and even more important to her, the lives of her friends.

Margaret returned carrying a tray laden with a gold-rimmed Lennox teapot, matching tea cups, and a dessert plate of cranberry walnut crunch cookies. The two women engaged in polite chit-chat for several minutes. When Grace finished her tea, Margaret brought the conversation to the point of the visit. "What can I do for you, dear?"

"I dropped an earring the night I was here and was wondering if I could look for it."

"An earring? I'm so sorry. I wish I had known. The house has been cleaned quite thoroughly since the party. I'm afraid anything on the floor would have been sucked up by the vacuum already."

Grace applied more pressure. "It's not that the earring is so valuable, but Alex gave it to me so it's very special. I understand there's not much hope of finding it, but if you don't mind my looking, it would make me feel so much better to know that I tried."

"Of course, dear. Do you have any idea which room you were in when you first noticed it missing?"

"I moved around quite a bit, even in the kitchen at the end when everything was so chaotic. Why don't I start by looking there?"

"Certainly."

Before beginning the hunt, Grace picked up her keys lying next to her on the sofa and dropped them into her purse, covertly pushing the number to speed dial Romy's cell phone. Without speaking or waiting for an answer, she pushed the end button to disconnect.

Her hostess led the way to the kitchen and the search for the missing earring, but was interrupted by a phone call. The moment she left the room, Grace unlocked the kitchen door and resumed searching.

Margaret returned immediately. "It's the head of Indiana's literacy campaign," she apologized. "They want me to serve as honorary chair for this year's fundraiser, and need to nail down a few items immediately. Do you mind?"

"Not at all. Take your time," Grace encouraged her smiling as she pictured Celina sitting in her office, impersonating the socialite.

"I'll be back in a few minutes," her hostess promised before returning to the phone in the family room.

When the sound of Margaret's footsteps ceased, Grace signaled out the window, and Romy tiptoed in carrying the hard drive of Margaret's original computer with the deleted files already restored to memory.

Once inside the study, Romy worked with as much speed as the need for silence would allow. She unscrewed the back of Margaret's new computer and exchanged hard drives. Next, Romy brought up Margaret's e-mail system.

"Dear Sergeant Crooke," she began to write. *"Thank you for the kindness and professionalism you demonstrated during our St. Patrick's Day party. Richard and I would like to show our appreciation by organizing a benefit to raise funds for bullet proof vests. Please review the attached spreadsheet detailing our plan, and let us know what you think. We look forward to hearing from you as soon as possible. Sincerely, Margaret Updike."* Romy then attached a section of incriminating files she had retrieved from the computer. "This ought to put him on the right track," she whispered pushing send before slipping back down the hall and out the back door.

Grace was hard at work searching the family room when Margaret joined her. "I'm sorry. That conversation took longer than I expected."

"No problem. What a compliment to be chosen as Honorary Chair of the Literary Campaign!" Grace enthused. "They couldn't have made a better choice."

"Thank you. I'm quite flattered to be asked. I believe Richard will be pleased as well. Any luck finding your earring?"

"No. You're probably right, it was cleared away." Grace looked around the room. "I sat on that sofa while people were dancing. I wonder if it could have fallen then."

"That's possible," Margaret answered, bending down to examine the sectional. "I don't see anything. Wait a minute. Grace, is this your earring?" She held up a gold loop with an emerald dangling from the center.

"That's it! I can't believe you found it. Thank you so much. The thought of losing this earring had me just sick."

"I'm glad we were able to find it." Margaret enthused. "Amazing, really. The cleaning lady was supposed to have vacuumed underneath all the cushions.

Two days later, Hamilton County sheriff deputies arrived at the mansion with a search warrant to confiscate all computer files. Mrs. Updike appeared very helpful and relaxed, even providing officers with her password. She wasn't as cooperative when they arrived the second time with a warrant for her husband's arrest.

Chapter Eighteen

On the second Monday in April, members of the Ladies of the Club met to discuss the final novel in Jan Karon's Mitford series. The snows had melted and invigorating rains had washed away the last vestiges of a worn-out winter. The breezy joy of spring unveiled a new season of life.

Inside the residence of Ms. Tamara Montgomery fresh tulips bloomed in ceramic vases and hyacinth-scented candles glittered against the light pine wood of early-American furniture. Old Forge table lamps and patchwork quilts added to the unpretentious ambiance that whispered home.

Celina looked around at the freshly painted walls and rearranged family room. "The house looks beautiful since you moved back in, Tamara."

"You don't think it looks too empty with all the furniture and pictures Greg took?"

"Not at all. It has a lighter, airier feeling," Celina approved.

"That's because the scum is gone," Romy piped up from her cushioned Windsor chair. Her friends shook their heads, but laughed.

Celina raised her hand high in blessing. "I declare this house scum-and-bonehead free."

"It does feel good to be back in my own home," Tamara admitted. "I can't believe Greg agreed to the terms you wrote up. How did you convince him to sign?"

"Let's just say we persuaded him it was in his own best interest," Celina hedged.

A bit uneasy with their evasiveness, Tamara probed further. "Was Grace okay with your method of persuasion?"

They all laughed, and Grace said, "I do have an important function in our group. I am the Club Conscience and Mistress of all Rules."

"You are very important to us," Romy assured her.

"Thank you," Grace smiled. "In answer to your question, I was fine with our method for encouraging Greg to do the right thing." Seeing the relief on Tamara's face, Grace grinned mischievously and added, "Although, in this case, I probably would have been okay with a little help from Vinny the Leg Breaker."

Lara slipped a folded piece of newsprint out of the front of her book. "There was an article in today's *Indi-*

anapolis Star I thought all of you might be interested in hearing." She began to read.

"Police followed the trail of an e-mail attachment to track down the systematic draining of Lincoln Township funds. The discovery of the theft led to new information regarding the murders of township employees Winston Dopplar and Cindy Patterson.

Detectives matched the ice pick used to the kill senior accountant to a silver set found in the walkout basement of the Updike mansion. Forensics also found traces of blood matching that of Dopplar on an antique Silver Cross baby carriage belonging to the Updike family.

Police originally suspected the superintendent of the crimes, and were on the verge of arresting him, when his wife confessed. Authorities were skeptical of the confession until Mrs. Updike revealed details of both homicides that only the murderer could have known."

"I like it when justice triumphs," Celina announced, with satisfaction in her voice.

"Me too," Grace agreed.

Even though the children were asleep upstairs, the weight of the topic caused Tamara to lower her voice.

"It does bother me that the township is out all that money paid to ghost employees," Tamara admitted, "but at least the stealing won't continue."

"They didn't get away with it," Grace protested. "They got caught. She's going to jail."

"But the schools are still out that money."

Romy scooped up a handful of peanut M & Ms. "Actually, the township isn't out any money. I put it back."

"You what?" Grace exclaimed.

"I transferred money from the Updikes' bank accounts back to township funds via the computer."

"You didn't!" Celina responded laughing.

"Do you mean to say you stole money from the Updikes and gave it to Lincoln Township Schools?" Exasperated with this latest law-breaking, Grace was ready for a fight. "I can't believe it! We're all going to end up in jail."

"She didn't steal it. She returned it," Celina defended their personal Robin Hood. "Think of it as enforced restitution."

"How much did you put back?" Lara asked.

"Every penny with prime rate interest compounded daily."

Celina smiled in admiration. "I'm impressed you know how to calculate the prime rate interest compounded daily. What a woman you are!"

The friends cheered, and then the room grew silent.

"What are you thinking about, Tamara?" Grace asked softly.

"I'm thinking about how lovely it is to relax in my

own home with my friends. So many women don't even have one good friend they can rely on. I have four. I am blessed by your friendship." Tamara raised her teacup in toast. "To the Ladies of the Club."

"To the Ladies of the Club," they chorused.